MOSTLY PERFECT

THE WOMEN OF
AMBROSE ESTATE

MOSTLY PERFECT

THE WOMEN OF AMBROSE ESTATE

HEATHER B. MOORE

Copyright © 2019 by Heather B. Moore
Print edition
All rights reserved

No part of this book may be reproduced in any form whatsoever without prior written permission of the publisher, except in the case of brief passages embodied in critical reviews and articles. This is a work of fiction. The characters, names, incidents, places, and dialogue are products of the author's imagination and are not to be construed as real.

Interior design by Cora Johnson
Edited by Kelsey Down and Lisa Shepherd
Cover design by Rachael Anderson and Steven Novak
Cover image credit: Deposit Photos #25592211

Published by Mirror Press, LLC

ISBN: 978-1-947152-71-7

Generations of secrets. An ancient curse.
Love has never been an option.

Lauren Ambrose has made a life for herself as a fledging artist, far from the ancient secrets and cobwebbed past of her family's historic estate in Texas. Generations of the Ambrose women have suffered at the hands of a curse, and the last place Lauren wants to spend time is at the Ambrose Estate, among the tragedies of the past. But when her grandmother, matriarch of the Ambrose fortune, requires Lauren to attend an urgent business meeting, she reluctantly travels home.

Nick Matthews is ready for a battle. Lillian Ambrose, co-founder of Ambrose Oil, has agreed to hear his investment idea, but no one has ever successfully partnered with the business tycoon. When he arrives at Ambrose Estate, prepared with weeks of research, the last person he expects to meet is Lauren, a dynamic and captivating woman with a past full of secrets. As Nick gets to know Lauren, he discovers she is mostly perfect for him, except for one, major drawback . . . The curse that has the power to destroy everything between them.

Lauren Ambrose's Genealogy

Ambrose sisters:
Sofia
Lauren
Emma
Amelia
Kendra
Katelynn

Lauren's Parents:
Poppy Ambrose Chambers
Randall Aaron Chambers

Grandparents:
Lillian Marie Ambrose Millet
Richard Jacob Millet

Great-Grandparents
Helen Elizabeth Ambrose Burton
Walter Charles Burton

Great-Great-Grandparents
Margaret Florence Thorne Ambrose
George Frederick Ambrose II

All female descendants are given the extra middle name of Ambrose.

1

LAUREN AMBROSE FANNED her face with her boarding pass as she stood at the curb in front of the regional airport. Next she lifted her long, wavy hair and did the same for her neck. She'd forgotten how humid Texas was near the Gulf of Mexico in the summer. Well, she hadn't forgotten, but the weather hadn't been on her mind when she'd received an urgent phone call from her Grandmother Ambrose the night before. Lauren was sure she'd pay for her rushed packing later, but for now, the taxicab was late, and every passing minute only made Lauren more worried.

Her grandmother had been cryptic about what was going on, but the insistence in her aged voice had left no room for argument. Was it her health? Something to do with the estate? Lauren rarely communicated with her sisters, or her half-sisters, Amelia, Kendra, and Katelynn. So she didn't even know they'd been called home too. Or her mother. Little chance of that. Her mother was on husband number five and living a life separate from her daughters.

A taxicab pulled up to the curb, and Lauren sighed in relief. She hoped the air conditioning would be working and she'd arrive in Ambrose more calm than she felt. Picking up her single suitcase, she headed toward the rear door of the cab. Just as she stepped off a curb, a man seemed to come out of nowhere. He reached the cab door first and opened it.

Lauren stared in disbelief. This guy was stealing her taxi.

"Excuse me, sir," she said, latching onto the open door as the man moved to load his carry-on into the trunk. "This is my taxi."

The dark-haired man turned to look at her.

Surprise showed in his hazel eyes. Lauren tried to keep her gaze steady, although she couldn't help but notice how this man looked like he belonged on one of those top ten sexy men posters. Her first thought was that he was an athlete of some sort—maybe a former athlete? His shoulders were plenty broad, and his arms and hands looked quite capable of doing athletic things. She guessed him to be in his early thirties, so maybe he was retired? And doing *what* in this small part of Texas?

His gaze focused on her, as if he was trying to comprehend what she'd said.

"This is the taxicab I ordered," she said again, curling her fingers around the door to demonstrate her ownership.

The driver climbed out of the car and looked at them both across the hood. "Nicholas Matthews?"

"That's me," the dark-haired man said, snapping his gaze to the driver. "And you're Sanchez?"

"Yes, sir," the cab driver said.

Lauren fumbled with her phone, trying to pull up the confirmation text she'd received from the cab company. Yep, there was the time and date . . . and . . . was today *Wednesday*? No, it was Tuesday. Heat flashed through her, and she released the door.

"Seems I've made a mistake," she said in a small voice, meeting Mr. Matthews's amused gaze. He was one of those . . . for lack of a better term, *pampered* guys. Expensive suit, a watch that must have costs thousands, and those shoes—definitely Italian leather. And she was totally checking him out. *Eyes up, Lauren.* "Sorry, I, uh . . . sorry."

She turned and hauled her suitcase back onto the curb. She was pretty sure Italian-leather-shoe guy was silently laughing at her. Now what? She'd probably have to wait an hour for another taxicab to come. The airport was small, and it wasn't like she could book a Lyft or Uber. And she hadn't wanted to bother with the hassle of a rental.

"Where are you headed, ma'am?" the man asked.

Lauren looked over at Mr. Nicholas Matthews—or whatever he went by.

Was he just being polite, or was he sincere?

"Ambrose," she said.

Mr. Matthews smiled. It was one of those smiles that probably secured him a lot of dates. If he was single, that was. No wedding ring in sight, but that didn't mean much in today's world. "It's on my way," he said. "How about we share the cab?"

Lauren blinked. What were the chances he was a creep? A good-looking, wealthy, polite creep with beautiful olive skin? And how was he not sweating to death in that suit of his? She glanced at the cab driver, who looked like he was okay with waiting for their decision since his meter was already on. The taxicab was from the same company Lauren had booked, and it was a reputable company. So . . . the taxi was safe.

The wild card was Nicholas Matthews.

She looked into his hazel eyes and decided he looked sincere.

"Okay." She rotated her suitcase and carried it down the curb again.

Mr. Matthews reached for the handle of her suitcase. "I've got it."

He smelled . . . expensive. Lauren's stomach did a little flip, but she immediately suppressed any wayward butterflies.

She decided not to argue with his offer to take the suitcase. The sooner she was inside the taxicab, the sooner she could cool off.

"Are you okay?" he asked in a smooth voice.

Lauren blinked. He was asking if she was *okay*? "Yeah, I'm fine. Why?" She hadn't meant to sound defensive, but it was too late to backtrack.

He didn't seem bothered by her sharp reply. "You look a little frazzled."

Frazzled? That was the least of it.

"This is an unexpected trip, that's all." She gave him a small, dismissive smile and moved past him. Then she slid into the back seat and pulled the door closed.

Moments later the taxi driver was seated, and Nicholas Matthews had settled into the front seat.

Yeah, he definitely smelled expensive. Subtle, though. Not too strong of a cologne, which made her wonder if it was body wash. Lauren fanned herself again. Maybe she should have sat in the front seat, closer to the AC vents. She pulled up the taxicab company website on her phone and canceled the scheduled pickup—for tomorrow.

As the driver merged onto the main road, he asked, "Where y'all from?"

Oh, good. A chatty driver. Lauren was not interested in chatting with the driver, or any other stranger. She wasn't antisocial or anything, but once she said her name and that she'd grown up on Ambrose Estate, she'd be treated differently. And not in a positive way.

Her grandmother was the known matriarch of Ambrose and the wealthiest woman in the county, possibly the entire state. Not even Lauren knew the exact extent of her grandmother's holdings. That was for her sister Sofia to keep track of. She was the new owner of the Ambrose Oil Company their grandmother had co-founded.

"I'm from San Diego," Nicholas Matthews told the driver.

Lauren's breath stalled. She lived in San Diego too . . . had the man been on her flight? She hadn't seen him, and she was pretty sure she would have noticed. She dug the earbuds out of her multicolored bag and clicked them into her phone, then slipped them on her ears. She didn't turn on any music, but maybe it would clue the driver into the fact that she wasn't going to play twenty questions.

"I've never been to San Diego," Sanchez said. "Although it sounds nice."

"Of all the places I've lived, San Diego has the best weather."

Lauren agreed, curious about how many places Nicholas Matthews had lived. She didn't want to be curious, but she was already listening.

"What do you do for a living?" the driver continued.

"I'm in acquisitions," Nicholas Matthews said. "How about you? Is this your full-time job?"

"Part-time for now."

During the rest of the ride to Ambrose, Nicholas Matthews took control over the conversation, asking the driver questions, which Lauren found interesting.

She exhaled as they passed the final sign on the road, indicating only five miles to go until they arrived in Ambrose. She peered out the window, debating where to tell them to drop her off. She didn't want them to take her onto the estate grounds. Then she had an idea.

"I'm at the bed-and-breakfast on the corner," Lauren said, taking out her earbuds.

The cab driver slowed the car, and Lauren pulled out a few bills from her wallet. She set them on the middle console between the two front seats as the cab stopped in front of the bed-and-breakfast. By the time she'd opened the door and climbed out, Nicholas Matthews had gotten out of the cab too.

With the driver busy lifting her case out of the trunk, Mr. Matthews said, "Are you sure you're okay?"

She looked up at him. Lauren was about five nine, and this guy had to be at least six three or six four. "It's been a long day, Mr. Matthews."

"Call me Nick," he said.

Lauren's first thought was that he had a mobster name, but that was ridiculous.

"I didn't get your name," he continued in that smooth voice of his.

"That's because I didn't give it out."

The edge of his mouth lifted, and he held out the money she'd just put onto the console. "I'll pay for the cab."

The driver set the suitcase next to her and went around the taxi to climb back in.

"Are you from around here?" Nick asked.

Now he wanted to ask questions? While standing outside the taxi?

"Something like that." She grasped the handle of her suitcase. Giving him a hint.

"If you need anything, give me a call." He pulled a business card out of the inner pocket of his suit coat and handed it to her.

He climbed back into the cab then, leaving Lauren to stare after him.

On the business card were only two things. His name and a phone number.

2

NICK MATTHEWS DIDN'T know why he'd offered to share a cab with Lauren Ambrose. He'd recognized her the second he stepped out of the airport and saw her standing on the curb. It wouldn't have been a good idea to introduce himself, even though he'd be meeting her in a more formal setting soon enough. Although the picture he had of the Ambrose family was several years old, there was no mistaking the woman was the second daughter of the family.

Second daughter and heiress to a billion-dollar holding company. Provided Lillian Ambrose, matriarch of the clan, and co-founder of Ambrose Oil, made the right decision. And that's what Nick intended on helping her do.

Nick didn't know what he'd expected coming face to face with one of the Ambrose women, but it wasn't Lauren. Her long hair had a wild, untamed look, as if she'd just come off a camping trip. And her clothing . . . not the classy designer look of her sisters, whom he'd done research on. In fact, he'd found very little about Lauren, since she wasn't part of any social media sites.

Her V-neck T-shirt was plain white, and the printed sarong skirt she wore hugged her curvy hips. Not that Nick had allowed himself to check out Lauren Ambrose. His clients were always off-limits. But he could appreciate a natural beauty, and Lauren definitely fit that mold. Her lake-blue eyes and dusky lips were free of any makeup. She didn't wear any jewelry, save for a silver chain necklace that disappeared beneath her shirt.

Nick loosened his tie and was tempted to shed his suit jacket, but he'd wait until he reached the house he'd rented for the month. "Always dress professionally," his father had told him more than once. And it had paid off well. At least, that's what Nick believed.

His father's funeral six months ago had driven Nick toward a nostalgia he'd never had when his father was alive. In fact, Nick found himself understanding his father's business practices more and more. And here Nick was . . . carrying out another tactic developed by his father, who believed that any business worth acquiring took more than studying numbers on a spreadsheet.

It took hands-on research. Which was exactly why Nick had come to Ambrose a full three days before his meeting with Lillian Ambrose. He had no doubt that she'd entertained venture capitalists before. And he knew that she'd turned down every acquisitions offer ever made. No matter the amount. It seemed that Lillian Ambrose valued other things above money. Which included her six granddaughters.

"Is this it?" Nick asked as the taxi driver pulled into a long driveway leading to an elegant two-story home.

"This is the address you sent to the company, sir."

"Very well," Nick said. The place would have to do. All he required was high speed internet, a stocked fridge, and a lot of privacy. He hoped this house wasn't on anyone's list to keep an eye on. Chatting with neighbors wasn't on his to-do list.

He paid the driver, then carried his suitcase to his new residence for the next thirty days, although Nick was hoping to be out of here much sooner than that.

3

Lauren tucked the business card that Nicholas Matthews had given her into her bag. With the odds and ends in her bag, the card would get lost in no time. There was no reason to call a perfect stranger for anything. And the sooner she arrived at Ambrose Estate, the better. Lauren pulled up the contacts on her phone and called William Shelton, chauffeur of her grandmother.

He picked up on the second ring. "Lauren?" His warm voice was good to hear. "Are you in town?"

"The cab dropped me off at the bed-and-breakfast," Lauren said. "Can you pick me up?"

"Sure thing," Shelton said, and she heard the questions in his voice. Questions he wouldn't ask. If there was one quality that could be attributed to Shelton, it was discretion.

That was probably why he'd kept his job at Ambrose for going on thirty years.

Lauren thanked him, then hung up. Next, she carried her suitcase to the bench in front of the bed-and-breakfast and sat down. She had at least ten minutes to wait. Which meant that about twenty minutes from now, she'd be in front of her grandmother, hearing what was going on.

Lauren exhaled. Getting here had been a whirlwind. No, she didn't have a boss to tell that she was going out of town, but she had to arrange with a neighbor to water her plants and feed Silver, an elusive cat that had adopted itself to Lauren a couple of years ago. The final phone call she'd made had been to Kevin. The man who had told her twenty-four hours ago that he was falling in love with her.

Lauren regretted letting things go so far with Kevin. She never dated anyone for more than five dates. After five dates, men wanted to get more serious. Wanted her to meet their families, go on a weekend vacation together, and talk about future plans.

But she'd been negligent with Kevin. She'd been irresponsible. She should have broken things off weeks ago. It was as if her grandmother's phone call had pulled her out of whatever rose-colored world she'd been living in. A world that didn't, and wouldn't ever, belong to her. For Lauren to let things with a man progress to an engagement and a marriage would be a death sentence. Literally.

The men who married Ambrose women died young. All of them.

All the way from her great-great grandfather, George Ambrose's early death, down to her own father, who had been only thirty-six.

Her mother had married multiple times, had even more boyfriends than Lauren could remember, and so as soon as possible Lauren and her sisters were out living on their own. Which was part of why Lauren didn't have much communication with any of her siblings. Different fathers, multiple homes, living under the shadow of what seemed to be a curse, didn't encourage much family affection.

None of her sisters or half-sisters had dared to marry.

A black Cadillac slowed in front of the bed-and-breakfast.

Lauren rose to her feet as Shelton climbed out. He crossed to her, limping as usual, his nearly bald head shining beneath the sun. Shelton's age had always seemed indeterminable, but Lauren guessed him to be in his mid-sixties.

"How are you, darlin'?" Shelton asked, stopping to grasp her hands.

Lauren squeezed his hands. "Fine. It's great to see you."

Shelton grinned his gap-toothed smile. "You too, doll."

He never held back on the endearments, and Lauren didn't mind them coming from him.

"Now, let me help you there," he said, turning to the suitcase.

"I've got it," Lauren said, picking it up. "Just open the trunk."

Once they were on the road, Lauren started with the questions. "Are any of my sisters here?"

"Sofia is, of course," Shelton said. "Mrs. Ambrose only requested that you and Sofia be present, since she's the owner, and you are the majority shareholder."

"So this is about business, then?" Lauren said. "Grandmother's health is all right?"

"She's still ticking," Shelton said, a smile in his voice.

When they turned onto the winding driveway that led through a copse of flowering trees to the estate house, Lauren felt both a sense of coming home and an increased anxiety about what this could all mean.

A sloping lawn led up to the stately mansion that had more rooms inside than anyone knew what to do with. Even when Lauren was a child, her grandmother had kept most of the rooms closed off. Lauren and her sisters had spent hours playing hide-and-seek or daring each other to go into one of the deserted rooms in the dark. Either that or the family graveyard that was behind the house.

Now, the mansion loomed before her, looking a bit run-down in the brightness of the afternoon. Shelton pulled around to the massive four-car garage—something her grandmother had added to when Lauren was a kid.

"I'll take in your suitcase if you want to go to your grandmother directly," Shelton said.

Lauren exhaled. "Okay, I'll do that. Thank you."

Shelton nodded, and Lauren climbed out of the car.

She walked around the front of the house by habit. The side entrance had always been reserved for the employees of the household. As Lauren stepped into the cool interior of the massive hall, with a crystal chandelier above, her gaze went directly to the curved staircase that led to the second floor, where her grandmother's suite occupied one of the wings.

The place smelled like a mix of furniture polish and dried lavender, bringing back more memories of her childhood. She wondered if the taxidermy animals were still in the library and if the dumbwaiter still creaked as it moved between the levels of the house.

She crossed the luxurious carpeting that was sun dappled with the afternoon light coming in through the high windows that followed the staircase. Then she headed up the stairs in the near silence, save for the grandfather clock ticking endlessly. By the time she reached the top of the stairs, voices reached her.

She heard more than one female voice, and Lauren could only assume Sofia was with their grandmother.

Lauren headed down the hall to find the French double doors to her grandmother's suite of rooms open a few inches. So Lauren pushed the door open. Sofia stood in front of the empty marble fireplace. Her beautiful, wavy hair fell elegantly over her shoulders, unlike Lauren's haphazard tumbled locks. Sofia's pale skin was delicate and almost ethereal. She was the beauty of the family. And in a damask reclining chair, her grandmother sat with an afghan draped over her legs.

At first glance, the scene might look tranquil, but Lauren knew that nothing about her grandmother was tranquil.

Sofia saw her first, and there was no friendly greeting or sisterly embrace.

"Hello, Lauren," Sofia said. "Glad you're here, because our grandmother is about to make a huge mistake."

Lauren's gaze cut to her grandmother—who smiled.

"Come here, dear," her grandmother said, as if Sofia hadn't spoken at all.

Lauren crossed to her grandmother, feeling her insides go soft at the loving expression on her grandmother's face. If there was one person in the world who Lauren could say truly cared about her, it was her grandmother.

Lauren grasped her grandmother's hands and bent to kiss her cool, papery cheek. The aroma of roses and Grandmother's favorite Prince Matchabelli perfume greeted her, and Lauren had no doubt that her grandmother was still taking rose-water baths each morning.

Lillian Ambrose might be a sweet-smelling, mild-expressioned woman, but she had a spine of steel and a heart that never wavered.

"Sofia arrived a couple of hours ago from Houston," her grandmother said. "I wanted to wait for your arrival so that I could tell you together, but it seems in my old age, I've lost a little of my resolve."

This was hard to believe, and Lauren only nodded. "It's okay. I'm just glad to see that you're healthy and not struck down with some mysterious illness."

Sofia scoffed but said nothing.

Her grandmother's clear blue eyes gleamed with amusement. "You thought I was calling from my deathbed to give you last words of wisdom?"

Lauren smiled, although now she realized how foolish that was. If her grandmother was dying, Sofia would have called her. She was the executor of the estate, after all.

"You were certainly mysterious on the phone." Lauren released her grandmother's hands and took the closest chair next to her.

"Well, you know how I feel about phone calls, dear," her grandmother said in a lowered voice. "Anyone could be listening."

Since her grandmother was a woman who'd had to claw her way up in a man's business world, Lauren had no doubt that there had been experiences that she knew nothing about. The proverbial glass ceiling was still in place for career women nowadays, but forty years ago, her grandmother had single-handedly grown her oil-rich land into a major contributor in the oil business. She invested her profits into other companies, namely pharmaceuticals, and the dividends continued to pay off.

"So . . ." Lauren prompted. "What's going on that's so important I needed to catch the first flight out of San Diego?"

"Your mother has hired a ghost hunter."

Lauren blinked. "Is that all?" Her mother had hired other ghost hunters in the past to rid the Ambrose estate of the death curse that affected all men married to Ambrose women. Was this time any different?

"It's a woman who's been on that television program," her grandmother said. "She's quite famous."

Lauren searched her mind for what her grandmother was talking about. Sure, she'd heard of TV series that went to sites of supposed hauntings . . .

"Granny," Sofia said. "That's not what's important about this meeting. Tell Lauren about the VC."

Lauren slowly turned her head to look at her sister. *VC* could mean only one thing. Her grandmother was in talks with a venture capitalist? One who warranted calling her two granddaughters home?

"You're going to sell out?" Lauren asked in a quiet voice. This was something her grandmother had sworn never to do—not in her lifetime—and according to the organizational structure of the company, as long as two out of the six granddaughters were alive, there was no way to sell off the company. Only Lillian Ambrose had the power to do that. Recently, Lillian had officially made Sofia the owner of the franchise, but Lillian still had her say as the co-founder of the organization.

"Partner," her grandmother said. "The VC has sent scientific research to me that indicates we might still have vast stores of oil on our lands. Modern technology will be able to locate it, and then the oil part of our company moves back into full production."

"And this VC . . ." Lauren started. "What's he asking?"

"That's why I want you two girls here," her grandmother said. "He sent over the details, and we'll spend tomorrow reviewing them. He's coming on Friday to meet with me, and I want you both in the meeting with your questions. Sofia is already set against it, and as the new owner of Ambrose Oil, her word is final. But I hope to dissuade Sofia from taking such a hard stance. Thus, we invited you, Lauren."

Lauren exhaled.

"He's a swindler, Granny," Sofia said. "I looked him up, and he takes over companies and crushes them. Turns them over to someone else, making money. He's nothing but a used-car salesman. He doesn't care about this land or our legacy."

Her grandmother was silent for a moment, but Lauren noticed how tightly she gripped the arms of her chair. "Our meeting is at nine a.m. Friday. I expect both of you to have reviewed all materials and be at the meeting."

Sofia crossed to the bank of windows and stared out across the winding gardens. "Nicholas Matthews should have stayed in San Diego," she muttered.

"What did you say?" Lauren asked.

When Sofia didn't answer, Lauren looked at her grandmother. "What's the VC's name?"

Her grandmother met her gaze. "Nicholas Matthews."

4

THE AMBROSE LIBRARY was quaint, and dust particles danced and twirled in the air in front of the bookcase Nick stood in front of. Apparently, this library hadn't digitalized any texts written by local historians, so literally the only way to read more about Ambrose Estate was to come to the library itself.

It was all a part of his research, though, and knowledge he wanted to have before his meeting tomorrow. He pulled out a slim volume with a faded blue cover. *The Unauthorized Biography of Lillian Ambrose.* Nick wondered if Mrs. Ambrose knew this book existed. He opened the cover and read the copyright. Ten years old and published by a press he'd never heard of.

He took the book to one of the tables by the window and sat down to thumb through it. Information about Lillian Ambrose was hard to come by, but before Nick had gotten his MBA, he'd majored in history. Research was kind of his forte, and he loved the chase for information and obscure details.

Nick skimmed the first chapter, which covered information he already knew about Lillian. Birth, parents, list of siblings, all long gone now. The second chapter provided nothing new. But he slowed his perusal on the third chapter, where the children of Lillian and her husband, Richard Jacob Millet, were introduced. The couple had had three children, two sons who'd died young, and a daughter named Poppy.

Nick leaned back in his chair and gazed out the window, not really seeing the small town street beyond. So many deaths, and all males. It was an interesting phenomenon. In fact, in his estimation, no Ambrose man had ever lived past thirty-nine. Nick had read plenty of historical legends and lore over the years, since they seemed to creep into every era and culture. But usually legends were created in order to explain away mysterious situations.

Nick turned to chapter four. Ah. There it was. The chapter was titled, "The Ambrose Curse." According to the unauthorized biographer, Mr. Richard Jacob Millet Ambrose had been a hard-headed, controlling businessman who believed that women belonged barefoot and pregnant. Upon his deathbed he made his wife promise to turn over the ownership of the company to his brother. He also forbade her to remarry.

Lillian Ambrose upheld the edict to not marry, but instead of contacting her brother-in-law or any other in-law, Lillian told no one of her husband's death. She acted as if he were still alive and running the oil business. She signed his name to every document and communicated through letters. And no one was the wiser. She even added a majority partner to the company—herself—then eventually added her granddaughters.

And now, Sofia was the named owner of Ambrose Oil, not even Lillian's own daughter, Poppy. Yet another mystery.

A movement to his left caught his attention, and he looked up to see a woman step out of one of the book aisles a few rows down. She wore earbuds and carried about five books. The woman's back was turned toward him as she moved to a table in the corner with a library computer, but her tumble-blonde hair and lithe movements gave her away.

Lauren Ambrose was in the library.

He could only see her partial profile, but there was no doubt. Those long lashes, dusky lips, her elegant neck, and her simple, feminine clothing. Her blouse was red and white, a loose bohemian style. Her skirt was long, with tiny red flowers, and reached her ankles. But even all the fabric couldn't hide her natural curves. She wore wedge sandals, and she crossed her ankles as she started leafing through one of the books on her tables.

Nick blinked, realizing he was staring. He'd been caught off guard, and he supposed he was curious as well. It was just ironic, that was all. Here he was reading about the Ambrose family, and a family member shows up at the same time.

Nick returned to the biography and started to read chapter six. It was a detailed description of how Lillian Ambrose grew her business and started investing in pharmaceuticals. All of this Nick knew, and his attention strayed again.

Lauren typed on the computer keyboard, and although Nick couldn't see exactly which searches she was typing in, she seemed to be googling for information. Numbers littered the screen, and Nick could tell she'd pulled up a financial site of some sort. She stared at the screen for a couple of moments, then she exhaled loud enough for Nick to hear and dropped her face into her hands.

Nick stilled. Was something wrong? His simmering curiosity upon seeing her was now burning at full heat. He watched . . . and waited. When she didn't move for several moments, he felt compelled to cross to her to see if she was all right. But he knew that wouldn't be a good idea. He should mind his own business. In fact, he should leave the library and not bother her at all.

Yet . . .

Lauren raised her head and picked up her phone. Then she answered it.

First, Nick was surprised she'd answer her phone in the quiet of the library. Second, he was immediately riveted to her words.

"Stop calling me, Kevin," Lauren said in a hushed voice. "No . . . It doesn't matter anyway . . . Things are over . . . I'm sorry if you felt like I led you on . . . I'm sorry . . . That won't make a difference . . . I'm hanging up now . . ."

She clicked something on her phone, then set it back on the table.

Nick didn't move. Now he'd feel terrible if she saw him and realized he'd heard everything.

He noticed the slight tremble of her hand as she used the mouse to exit out of the screen and type in another search. She continued to click through several links and didn't appear to be focusing on one particular thing but endlessly scrolling. Too fast to be reading anything or even skimming.

Maybe Nick could escape down the aisle and she wouldn't even notice. Or maybe ... he could pretend that he'd just arrived at the library and hadn't been sitting there. But something propelled him to stand. He walked over to Lauren, knowing he shouldn't, but his legs weren't obeying his mind.

She looked up, and her lips parted in surprise. Her blue eyes took in the whole of him, which made Nick feel uncommonly warm.

"Hi, we meet again," Nick said, lamely. Smoothness with women had never been a weak spot for him, but right now he felt like a fish out of water because of the guilt pounding through his chest. Although he couldn't exactly explain what sort of guilt that was.

Instead of returning his greeting, Lauren Ambrose rose to her feet and took a step back. Then she raised her hand and pointed at him. "You need to leave. Now. We don't want you here, and if you harass my grandmother one more minute, I'm filing a lawsuit."

Nick was speechless. The vehemence in her voice was genuine, and the fury in her eyes burned through his chest. "Lauren ..." he began.

But she cut him off and moved closer now, bringing with her the scent of wildflowers. "You don't know me or my family, and men like you only care about one thing. Yourselves. My grandmother might have invited you to present your proposal, but I'm *uninviting* you."

She was close enough that Nick noticed she had at least two different color blues in her eyes, and she was still wearing that silver chain, which once again disappeared beneath the neckline of her blouse.

"Can we talk?" Nick asked. "I'm happy to answer any questions."

"No," she shot out. She moved away now, and with a final parting look at him, she hurried off. Leaving her books behind.

Nick debated whether he should chase after her. But through a small-town library? And then what? His gaze cut to the table where she'd been sitting. The titles of the books she'd been looking through were like neon signs. *Mergers and Acquisitions. The History of Venture Capitalism. The Oil Industry of the 90s and Beyond.*

Then his eyes connected to the computer screen. His company's annual financial reports were staring back at him.

She'd been doing research, all right. *On him.*

5

LAUREN DIDN'T KNOW where she was going, but the last person she wanted to see, or speak to, was Nicholas Matthews. Her cell phone buzzed through the fabric of her bag, and she dug around inside of it, then pulled out her phone. Kevin was calling. Again.

Now she was angry. Guilt for not breaking things off with him sooner was no longer plaguing her. Yeah, she'd liked him plenty. But now . . . he was only annoying her. The man couldn't take no for an answer, and she'd only now realized that his personality was pushy all the way around. She knew if she went back through her call and texting log that she'd find that they'd been in contact multiple times a day over the past month of dating. He'd been overwhelming from the beginning, and Lauren had let his attention flatter her.

Now that she was out of the library, she didn't need to have a cryptic conversation with him. And that thought brought her to a stop near the town monument, where a statue of an Alamo fighter rose out of a waterless fountain.

Had Nicholas Matthews overheard her conversation? She hadn't seen him in the library when she'd arrived.

Her phone stopped ringing, then it started up again.

Sofia.

This call Lauren needed to answer. "Hi."

"Where are you?" Sofia asked.

"Just left the library."

"What did you find out?"

"That Matthews Capital and Holdings is a major shareholder of our grandmother's company."

Sofia cursed, and Lauren couldn't agree more.

"Tell me what that means exactly," Lauren said. Sofia was the business brain out of the sisters. Lauren felt accomplished if she got her taxes submitted on time each year.

"It means . . ." Sofia said in a slow voice. "That he has significant influence over our grandmother. And if she doesn't agree, or at least compromise with his suggestions, then he could ultimately sell his shares and hurt us. Horribly."

Three years ago, their grandmother had taken the business public. Investors had put up money to increase the value of the stock, which only had a ripple effect, driving it up even more. At least that's how Sofia had explained it to Lauren.

"So, worst case, he sells his twenty-three percent, and the stock dips a couple of dollars?"

Sofia sighed. "More likely it will lose fifty percent of its value."

Which meant multimillions.

"I feel like we're being cornered," Lauren said.

Sofia laughed, but it wasn't a happy laugh. "Now you know a small level of my anger toward this entire situation."

When Lauren hung up with her sister, she wandered around the fountain. The town was quiet this morning, and hot. She guessed that most people were on their summer vacations. She sat on the edge of the fountain. Kevin's number buzzed her phone again, and this time she answered.

"Please stop calling, Kevin," she said. "I don't want to have to block your number."

He chuckled. "Thanks for the friendly greeting. I think I deserve a better answer than you've given me. You know I treated you right. I paid for dinners, I brought you flowers, I even invited you to my grandfather's eightieth birthday."

Yes, that invitation had been what told Lauren that she had let things go too far. Had allowed Kevin's charming personality to make her forget where she'd come from and what happened to the men who married into her family. Although, Kevin wasn't being particularly charming anymore. And how could she tell him she was literally saving his life?

"We're good together," he said, his tone softening. "Come on, babe. We can slow things down if you want; that's fine with me. But I'd be lying if I didn't tell you that I've fallen for you. I know without a doubt that you're the woman for me. And I want to be the man for you."

Lauren looked up at the bright-blue sky. How did this happen to her?

"Babe," Kevin said. "Would it really be so hard to imagine a future with me? Maybe a kid, or two. We could live wherever you want."

Lauren swallowed against her suddenly dry throat. This was going way too far. "Kevin . . . I told you, it's not you, it's me. Blame *me*, whatever you want, but my mind isn't going to change."

Another laugh, and this one was more bitter than the first. "You have no problem trampling over my heart, I guess. I'm not stupid, Lauren. I know you've got your fancy family, and you think I'm just a simpleton, working construction. But believe me, I'm a real man, and I don't need a tux to prove it."

Lauren blew out a careful breath. She'd never told Kevin anything about her roots. "What are you talking about? What does wearing a tux have anything to do with you or me?"

"I googled you," he said. "And much to my surprise, I found that you've kept a lot of things from me. Care to explain?"

Lauren's face heated. "When did you google me, Kevin?"

He paused. "A couple of weeks ago."

But the hesitation in his voice told Lauren that he was lying.

"Was it before you came to my book signing, where you picked me up?" she said. A few months ago, she'd been featured in an American artist collection that was produced into a book. Three of her paintings had been selected, and Lauren had gone to the multi-artist event to sign books. Kevin had introduced himself to her as a fan of her work. "Because you said you had seen my work in a magazine and were a fan of mine before we even met. So you had plenty of time to find stuff out about my family."

He didn't answer.

Which was an answer in and of itself.

"If you know so much about me, you should also know that I live my own life," she continued. "Not one dictated by my family. I haven't touched my inheritance and probably never will. My will is written, and my shares will go to a select group of charities. So if you were thinking that you could marry a wealthy heiress, then you've got it all wrong."

"You're seriously a b—"

Lauren clicked END on her phone. Her hands were shaking and her eyes burning with tears as she turned off her phone completely. Yeah, she'd screwed up, but Kevin was way out of line.

"Hey, are you okay?"

It was *his* voice. Nicholas Matthews.

Could this day, this week, get any worse? She closed her eyes and didn't make an effort to wipe the tears that had escaped to her cheeks.

Footsteps moved closer—footsteps that she hadn't heard approach the fountain in the first place.

He said nothing else, but she knew he was still there. She could smell that expensive cologne. She thought with bitter irony how Nicholas Matthews was probably the only single man on the planet who wouldn't need to marry for money—he had plenty of his own.

Sure enough, when she looked over, those hazel eyes were watching her. Nicholas—or Nick—stood with his hands in his pockets, gazing down at her. Did he have no sense of privacy?

"Did you follow me?" she asked. Gone was her distress over Kevin, only to be replaced by a faint sense of panic.

"Not exactly," he said. At least he wasn't wearing a full suit, although he did have on a tie and an expertly pressed pinstripe shirt. His sleeves were rolled up a couple of times, and his dark silver watch gleamed against his olive skin. "I was headed to my car and saw that you seemed upset."

She didn't blink. Neither did he. There was no doubt this man was used to getting his way, whether it was because of his *GQ* looks or his mass of wealth.

When she didn't respond, he said, "Look, can we go somewhere and talk? Get a cold drink at the café or something?"

Lauren was about to refuse, but she *had* come here to research Nicholas Matthews and his company. What better way than to speak to the man himself?

Besides, he looked genuinely concerned . . . maybe it was because he undoubtedly knew she was a key influencer in whatever her grandmother would decide. Or maybe there was a bit of a human side to him.

"Okay," she said, surprising herself.

She'd definitely surprised him. His brows rose, and the edges of his mouth lifted.

"Great."

She grasped her bag and pulled it on her shoulder, then stood. Moving past him, she headed to the street corner where the café was situated. Nick walked alongside her, not saying anything, his hands still in his pockets. She wondered what he'd been doing at the library in the first place.

As she reached the door to the café, he stepped ahead of her and opened the door. She had to pass by him, and she tried not to breathe in his scent, one that she was now familiar with. Which was a ridiculous notion. She barely knew the man, yet he was already working his way into her senses.

The café was empty save for the teenager working the counter, someone whom Lauren didn't know. She ordered a lemonade, and Nick ordered water, surprising her. Lauren crossed to the small table closest to the bank of windows and took a seat.

He folded himself into the chair across from her, seeming to dwarf the seating arrangement. Lauren guessed that he didn't make visiting small-town cafés a habit. Still, he seemed at ease, which only made Lauren more nervous. At least the temperature inside the café was cool, and she was cooling off bit by bit. Breathing easier. Feeling less like she was on a roller-coaster.

She would find out as much as she could about this man, then come up with a way to use it against him.

6

It took all of Nick's willpower not to remove his tie and loosen his collar. Another mantra of his father's was to always look professional. It gave off the vibe of being serious and capable, not to mention provided the competitive advantage.

But sitting across from Lauren Ambrose was throwing Nick off-center. Yes, the café was much cooler than the warming morning outside, which was why he suggested they come here. He needed a cup full of ice but had opted for water instead. Another mantra from his father—always order water when with a client. It makes you more trustworthy.

Nick wanted to lean forward and lift that silver chain of Lauren's to find what she wore so close to her heart. Instead, he drank from his ice water, relishing in the coolness slipping down his throat. Then he folded his hands on the table, if only to prevent the temptation to fidget.

Lauren had yet to meet his gaze as she stirred the lemonade that she'd ordered. Her mesmerizing movements as she circled the straw, slowly rotating the ice, were hard to look away from. Her blonde hair tumbled about her shoulders, and her dusty-pink lips were slightly pursed as if she was in deep thought.

Was she thinking about her grandmother's company? Him? Or maybe the man she'd been talking to on the phone? Nick had heard enough of the conversation, or more accurately, argument, to suspect it was a boyfriend. Or maybe an ex-boyfriend by now.

"Do you need me to break some kneecaps for you?" he asked in a low tone.

Lauren's gaze snapped up, her blue eyes wide. "What are you talking about?"

He swallowed. "That man you were talking to . . . Kevin?"

Pink stained her cheeks. Nick was fascinated. It was as if her emotions played out right on her face. She was staring at him, and he didn't know if that meant she was embarrassed, angry . . . ? "*Is* he your boyfriend?"

She shook her head. "Not anymore." Then her gaze dropped again. "I don't have boyfriends. I mean . . ." She licked her lips.

Nick took another long swallow of his ice water. He didn't believe she was faltering for words; it was more like she was avoiding telling him something. Because it was too personal?

He set down his glass. "I know about the curse."

She went absolutely still, and he waited as the sounds of the café hummed around them. The air conditioning, the low music, a car passing outside.

Finally, she raised those lake-blue eyes to meet his gaze. In them, he saw something like relief, which made him even more curious.

"Then you know why none of my sisters have married," she said in a voice tinged with resignation. "And you know why there's no point in me having a boyfriend, because that only leads to something more serious. Which I can't give."

"So you believe in the curse?" he asked in a careful tone.

A slight wrinkle appeared between her brows as she studied him. "I'm thirty years old, Mr. Matthews. I've never dated a man more than a few weeks. I only come back to Ambrose once or twice a year, and that's because my grandmother insists. But even if I never returned to Ambrose, I'd never forget who I am or where I came from. Whether I can explain the untimely deaths of every male member of our family as a curse or something else, the fact remains that it's true. As evidenced by the number of gravestones behind the estate home."

Nick had read through all of those names in the book at the library. "What about your mother?" he asked. "Her current husband is alive."

Perhaps his days are numbered too."

Nick leaned forward, keeping his voice low. "Maybe it's the land that's cursed, then, not the matrimonial connection?"

"The Ambrose women *are* the land, and the land is part of the Ambrose women," she said. "There's no division between the two."

Nick wasn't convinced, but he could see Lauren was, so he needed to tread carefully. It was, after all, a series of bizarre coincidences. All those males dying young. "Is that why you dumped Kevin?"

"That's why I *dated* Kevin," she said. "He was never my ideal anyway, so I knew it wouldn't be too hard to leave when the time came."

Interesting. "What was his response when you told him about the curse?"

That line between her brows appeared again. "I've never told any man about the curse," she said. "No one would believe me, so why bother? There are plenty of other reasons to end a relationship."

"True." Nick couldn't argue with that. He was the perfect example of ending relationships. It wasn't that there weren't amazing women out there who would make great partners and wives; it was more that he never trusted their motivations. Money had perhaps ruined that for him.

But he was thinking of what she'd said about Kevin not being her ideal. Which meant Nick was now wondering what her ideal *would* be . . . He took another drink from his water glass. Lauren still hadn't tried her lemonade.

"You've never met a man you thought could break the curse?" He didn't know how she'd react to his question, but he hadn't expected a smile.

His lungs felt weird. She was a beautiful woman, there was no doubt about that, but her smile . . . it was enough to make him forget why he'd invited her to chat in the first place. Lauren Ambrose needed convincing that her grandmother's company would be better off partnering with him.

"No, Mr. Matthews," she said in a rather breathless tone. "I've never met a man who's given me any reason to believe he could be the exception to a decades-old curse." The way her eyes gleamed told him she was teasing him.

He held back his own smile. "Is that because you haven't met your ideal man yet?"

She dropped her gaze and leaned forward to sip from the straw.

Nick loosened his tie. For once, he'd make an exception.

"I don't think ideal really exists, do you?" She leaned back in her chair, surveying him.

How did he answer that? His own parents' marriage had ended about ten years ago, but strangely enough they'd stayed friends. *Best friends.* His dad had said more than once that he loved the woman he'd married, but they were better apart than together. Neither of his parents had remarried or even dated. His mother ran a literary magazine that brought in no money, but she didn't seem to mind. She ran fundraising events that raised money for literacy programs in California, then she'd match the donations with her own.

He tried to think of other marriages, or relationships in general, that seemed ideal. "I believe you're right," he said at last.

"Does that mean you're not married?"

He chuckled, and she smiled fully at him. "Me and marriage don't agree."

She shifted forward, resting her elbows on the table. "Oh, there's a curse in your family?"

He scoffed, but his smile stayed on his face. "I think money could definitely be considered a curse, at least for some people."

"Well, you could try dressing down once in a while, and maybe you'll avoid the gold-digging women."

Nick stared at Lauren. Then he ran a hand through his hair. "That was blunt."

"Seriously, Mr. Matthews," she said. "I don't think I've seen that much starch in a shirt since the nineties. And that bling on your wrist. Really? And you're probably the first man to wear eight-hundred-dollar shoes in Ambrose."

Nick blinked. Had she really said all that to him? He looked down at his shoes and tapped his foot. "What's wrong with my shoes?"

She started laughing.

Her laughter was beautiful, just like the rest of her, but not when it was at his expense. He had one idea that might solve this situation.

He had the sudden urge to kiss that sassy mouth of hers. Which was completely ridiculous.

To top it off, her cheeks were stained pink again. "Sorry, I tend to say things, then think later. I think we've gotten way off topic here. And I'd appreciate it if you'd tell me why you want to meet with my grandmother." She gave a little shrug. "Blunt again."

Her abrupt change of topic shouldn't have been throwing him off-kilter, but it was. He exhaled and rested his forearms on the table. "I'm not at liberty to discuss specifics without your grandmother's presence, but I'm not the typical venture capitalist. So you know, I'm not going to take over and restructure. I'm more interested in expansion, but in the right way. There are areas of your family's company that have been neglected, and with recent advances in technology, I've discovered a few things that could be capitalized on."

"What happens to your shares if my grandmother turns you down?" she asked.

Blunt again. "Nothing."

She raised her brows. "BS."

He raised his brows. "I'm a straight shooter, Lauren."

Were her cheeks pink again because he'd called her by name, or was it something else?

"You'll sell, I know it," she said. "Maybe not all at once, but eventually, bit by bit."

"I'll do what's in the best interest of Matthews Capital and Holdings, but I can promise that no changes will ever be made without a thorough analysis of all possible outcomes and the viability of each."

By Lauren's expression, he knew that his vagueness wasn't impressing her.

"How does it feel to threaten an elderly woman?" Lauren said, her tone hard.

Now they were back to square one. "Business is just that . . . business."

Lauren's blue eyes were stormy. "Not to my grandmother. It's her life. Her pride. Her *family*. You destroy that, and you destroy her."

7

SO WHAT IF Lauren had walked out on Nicholas Matthews twice in one day? He was a bloodsucking, pompous, interfering . . . she was too mad to think of more adjectives. The tight feeling in her stomach only hardened as she walked back to Ambrose Estate, following the overgrown path she hadn't been on for years. And it appeared no one else had either.

Nick was going to wreak havoc on all that she knew and loved. Yes, she loved Ambrose Estate. She loved what her grandmother stood for. Lauren didn't necessarily want to work for the company like her older sister did or be involved in the day-to-day operations, but she was proud to be an Ambrose.

Just because she hadn't told Kevin, or any of her other dates or various friends over the years, anything about her heritage, didn't mean that she wasn't going to defend it at all costs. Lauren really had nothing to lose by going against Nicholas Matthews et al. Her laughter bubbled up with bitterness in her throat.

As Lauren stepped around a rather prickly bush, her cell rang. *Sofia.* Lauren was tempted to wait until she returned to the coolness of the house before answering, but her nerves were only coiling more and more.

"Sofia," Lauren said. "You won't believe who I just talked to."

"Who?" Sofia asked, although she didn't sound amused or in the mood to play a guessing game.

Lauren told her sister about seeing Nicholas Matthews in the library. She mentioned nothing about running out on him and then the subsequent call with Kevin. She simply skipped to the latter part. "He said he wanted to go to the café, have a drink, then talk."

Sofia groaned. "And you went, didn't you?"

"To gather information," Lauren replied, defending herself. "The more we know about our enemy, the better—"

"Lauren, what drink did he order?" Sofia asked.

"What does that have anything to do with it?"

"Lauren," she deadpanned.

"Water."

Sofia sighed into the phone. "He's playing you, Lauren. Let me guess, he asked *you* questions most of the time."

Lauren thought back. Her heating neck had nothing to do with the intermittent shade of the forest that did little to protect her from the rising temperature. Now that she thought about it, Nick had asked her a lot of questions. Personal questions.

"That's what I thought," Sofia continued. "He's figuring you out. Finding your weaknesses. Assessing your strengths."

Lauren swallowed against the dryness of her throat. "Unbelievable."

"Where are you?" Sofia asked.

"Walking through the Sleeping Beauty forest," Lauren said. It was what they'd called this patch of land when they were kids. What used to seem like imposing tress and foliage when Lauren was a child now resembled miserable weeds and wild bushes.

"You're such a hillbilly," Sofia said, but there was a note of affection in her voice. The first that Lauren had heard since her return.

"Just keeping out of the way of the smarter ones in the family," Lauren said.

Sofia scoffed. "You aren't fooling anyone hiding out in San Diego behind your paintings. I just don't get why you didn't see through Nicholas Matthews. Is he good-looking or something?"

"No!" Lauren choked out. "And what would that have anything to do with this anyway?"

"Ha." Sofia sounded way too triumphant. "You always were a sucker for good-looking men. Just like Mom, though not quite as spontaneous."

"Seriously? You're going to go there?" As annoyed as Lauren felt, she knew there was a grain of truth in her sister's words. Lauren was a romantic and the very definition of hopeless, because she literally had no hope.

What had Nick said? There was no such thing as ideal.

"How good-looking is he?" Sofia prompted with a laugh. "On a scale of one to ten?"

"Ten being *what*? A male model?"

"If he's a straight male model, then yeah, Calvin-Klein-hot is a ten."

Lauren mulled it over as she thought about his hazel eyes and flash of a smile. "He's a nine."

"Wow," Sofia said. "You're in trouble."

Lauren stepped out of the thicket into the sun. Perspiration had formed along her hairline, and she lifted the heaviness of her hair from her neck. "No, we're both going to be in trouble if he sells his shares."

Sofia went silent at that. "Maybe you can use your womanly charms on Mr. Handsome?"

"No way," Lauren said. "When you see him, you'll know that this guy will see through about anything." Besides, it seemed that Lauren was obviously quite dense. Sofia had picked up on what Nick was all about instantly. Lauren hadn't even realized that Kevin had ulterior motives to date her.

Nick was right. Money was a curse. There was a reason that Lauren hadn't divulged her net worth to anyone outside of her family.

"I'll be at the house soon," Lauren said, and after she hung up with her sister, she couldn't help but wonder about Nick's personal life. Her research so far had been about his business holdings.

But Lauren didn't head straight into the house. Instead she passed by the set of garages and walked around to the family graveyard behind the house. It was a decent walk from the house, and most of the way was shaded by sycamore trees.

As children, she and her sisters had dared each other to run to the wrought-iron gate and back without stopping. At night.

When their grandmother caught them, they all got a good scolding. She said it was disrespectful to the dead, and even the surrounding grounds were hallowed. Now, Lauren could see the same wrought-iron gate beyond a row of hedges as she approached. She swallowed against the lump that always formed in her throat around cemeteries.

Beneath the earth lay lost dreams and forgotten lives. It was strange to think that only the names etched upon the headstones and a bit of family lore remained of entire lives lived. Well, not entire lives . . . lives that had been cut short.

Lauren unlatched the gate and pushed it open. It swung open smoothly, and that was probably due to the immaculate care of the gardener, Reggie. Nothing was overgrown but carefully tended throughout the small plot. At the base of each headstone, no matter the age, were perennials in various states of growth and blooming. Beneath the sun's heat, they seemed wilted, but by the time evening rolled around, they'd regain their robustness.

Lauren crossed first to her father's headstone. It was an elegant spire, and *Randall Aaron Chambers* was scripted above the dates of his birth and death. Added to the headstone were the words:

Loved by all who knew him—especially his girls,
Sofia, Lauren and Emma.

He had been born in Baton Rouge and grew up to become a navy pilot. Their mother met him in college. His too-early death came when he was flying for the Blue Angels and died during an air show in a mid-air crash.

Lauren rested her hand on the stone, and the coolness sent a rash of goose bumps across her arms. Her memories of her father had grown fuzzy over the years, since he'd died when she was three years old, Emma was a baby, and Sofia only five. Lauren remembered him in uniform. Her favorite image of him was wearing navy whites with those medals.

She stood there for several moments, gazing at her father's name, then she finally dropped her hand and moved to the next headstone. Her uncle Robert. Dead at twenty-eight.

Next was her grandfather's, which was partially in the shade and enjoyed a riot of planted flowers at the base. *Richard Jacob Millet.*

Here was the proof that she'd told Nick about. He hadn't seemed dismissive or bothered that she believed in the curse. He'd seemed . . .

interested. And he'd listened intently. Which was a different experience for Lauren. Although according to Sofia, he was only keeping control of the conversation.

Lauren sighed as she walked back to the gate. So what if a man did believe in the curse along with her? There would still be no future in any of her relationships. Sometimes the loneliness was so acute that she didn't fault her mother her multiple marriages and refusal to return to Ambrose. Lauren knew she could never truly stay away from Ambrose. The land, the house, and everything associated with it pulsed through her like a slow heartbeat.

Kevin, or any other man, would never trump her attachment to her heritage. Or her grandmother.

Thinking of her grandmother only made the agitation return. Tomorrow Nicholas Matthews would be at Ambrose Estate, pitching his idea. And Lauren had a feeling that their lives were about to change.

8

Nick had left early enough to walk, but he'd miscalculated the time it would take to follow the road into Ambrose Estate. And he hadn't planned on the rain. All in all, it was a nice break from the two days of heat he'd endured, but his shoes would be worse for the wear.

And yes, they were Italian leather. In his defense, they were extremely comfortable and made walking two miles not a big deal. But the words of Lauren Ambrose seemed to echo through his mind. In fact, he'd replayed what she'd said, both in the library and then later at the café, multiple times in his mind.

When the house came into view, at the end of a very long lane, Nick paused to take in the sight. The three-story mansion was beautiful and stately, and the lawn leading up to it was immaculate. Formal gardens graced both sides of the house. But the closer he grew to the house, the more he began to notice some wear and tear. A place this size must take an incredible amount of upkeep, and from what Nick knew, Lillian Ambrose was a very busy woman.

Nick walked up the wide steps that led to a smaller lawn, and he followed the flagstone path to the imposing double front doors. He rang the bell, then stood back and brushed droplets off his suit coat. He ran a hand over his hair. It was damp, but not too bad.

The front door opened, and Nick was surprised to see Lauren at the door. He supposed he'd expected a more formal greeting, from a maid. Lauren's expression was hard to read, but she said in a soft voice, "Hello, Mr. Matthews."

"Nick," he said, although he doubted she'd obey. "How are you?"

Her gaze moved from his face to his damp clothing, and the faintest smile touched her lips. "You walked?"

"I did." He wasn't sure why, but he felt like smiling when her blue eyes connected with his again.

"You're wet."

His mouth twitched. "I am."

"Come in, come in," she said in a rush. "I'll get you a towel and something . . ." She glanced down. "For your feet."

"A towel would be fine," he said, following her into the grand entrance. "I don't need anything for my feet."

The line appeared between her brows, one that was familiar to him now.

"At least take your jacket off," she said. "The air conditioning will freeze you."

That he doubted, but he didn't complain as she moved closer and reached for the lapels of his suit coat. He watched her with amusement as she took upon herself the task of helping him out of his jacket. He thought he'd detected a faint pink on her cheeks that hadn't been present when she opened the door, but it faded soon enough.

Lauren smelled sweet, like a mixture of wildflowers and honey, and he wondered if it was her perfume or perhaps a lotion. Her hair was pulled into a twist at the nape of her neck, giving him full view of the elegance of her neck. And she wore a plain navy dress, high-necked and falling in a gentle sweep just above her knees. Well, nothing could be plain on Lauren, but he had the feeling that she'd borrowed this dress, since it was so different than anything he'd seen her in so far.

Lauren busied herself draping his jacket over a hall chair, then she said, "I'll be back in a moment. Sorry for the delay."

"I'm the one who should be apologizing for showing up wet."

She took another glance at him before turning away and heading into a room off the main hallway. He watched her walking away in those navy high heels of hers. While she was gone, he quickly checked his phone for any email updates.

He heard Lauren's heels before he saw her again. She walked toward him, carrying a towel.

"Are you sure you don't want a . . . sweater . . . or something?"

"I don't think a sweater of yours would fit me." He wiped the towel across his face and neck.

She exhaled. "I meant something from Shelton, our chauffeur," she said. "He has an apartment above the garages."

"No, thank you," he said. "My jacket took the worst of it."

"And your shoes."

They both looked at his shoes. He bent and dried his shoes with the already damp towel.

"I can put this away," he said when he finished.

But Lauren took the towel. "No, I've got it. Do you want something hot to drink? Warm you up?"

"I'm not cold," he said.

She didn't look entirely convinced, but she glanced away first from their locked gazes. "Well then, I'll be back in a moment, then we'll head to the library. My grandmother and sister are waiting there."

Nick nodded. "Thank you." As she disappeared again, he moved to a bank of paintings. They looked decades old, and he realized that one of the smaller ones was of Lauren as a young girl. At least he thought it was her. The cherubic four or five-year old sure looked like a precursor to the beauty that was Lauren. Yes, he had no problem recognizing her beauty. Many women were beautiful, and it wasn't something that would throw him off his agenda.

She seemed to be as unlucky in love as he'd been, although for her, it had been more out of fear. For him, it had been lack of sustained interest. Why his thoughts were so convoluted, he didn't know. The last thing he needed in this meeting was to be distracted by all that was Lauren Ambrose.

"This way, then," she said, and he turned to see her walk into the hall.

She didn't approach but waited for him to join her. Then she led the way to an austere library with floor-to-ceiling shelves of books and two blue-eyed women staring him down.

Out of the two sisters, Sofia Ambrose was the classic beauty, but with Lauren in the room, Sofia's features were almost porcelain and cold. Lauren radiated fluidity and warmth. And Mrs. Lillian Ambrose?

She was elegant like both of her granddaughters, but her dark hair was silvered with gray.

Mrs. Ambrose was dressed in a deep-green-colored dress, and she didn't rise as Nick approached but stayed seated in the high-backed chair before the empty fireplace.

"Good morning," Nick said, holding out his hand. "It's nice to finally meet you in person."

Mrs. Ambrose appraised him, her blue eyes open and curious, before she lifted her hand to shake his. Her hand was thin and would have been frail on any other elderly woman, but Mrs. Ambrose had a firm grip.

"I see you've met Lauren," Mrs. Ambrose said, her tone low and smooth. "This is my eldest granddaughter, Sofia, new owner of Ambrose Oil."

Sofia stepped forward and extended her long fingers. Nick shook her hand, finding it cool to the touch, not surprising from her. The woman's eyes seemed to bore right through him, possibly reading his every thought and intention. Nick knew of her veterinarian degree from Texas A&M and that she'd been an effective board member of Ambrose Oil Company. He just hoped she'd be as open-minded as her grandmother. Lauren, too. Especially Lauren.

"You walked?" Sofia said, as observant as her sister.

"I did."

"We can drive you back to wherever you're staying after the meeting," Sofia said, revealing her practical side.

"I might take you up on that if the rain hasn't let up."

"Oh, it won't let up, Nicholas," Mrs. Ambrose cut in. "We'll be enjoying it all day." Her voice was laced with humor, but Nick wasn't fooled. The woman was watching his every move.

Nick glanced around the room. There was a large credenza and several smaller end tables but no table that would fit all of them. "Should I set up at the desk?" he asked.

"Oh no," Mrs. Ambrose said. "We don't stand on ceremony here. You can sit in that chair."

Nick turned to look at the chair she'd indicated. A leather upright.

He scanned for any white space on a nearby wall so that he could show his PowerPoint, but the wallpaper was an etched brocade design of tan and gold. Besides, the closest wall was filled with miniature paintings that he had yet to examine.

He exhaled and made a decision. "Very well," he said. "I've brought several graphs to show, and I can also email them over."

Mrs. Ambrose simply nodded, so Nick sat down after Lauren and Sofia settled in chairs near their grandmother.

He pulled his laptop out of his computer bag and powered it on. He went through each slide, explaining the new oil-finding technology and then showing them the graphs that displayed the initial investment and the dividends it would bring in over the next eighteen months.

"Wait," Sofia said. "You're saying we can make back the cost of the equipment within eighteen months?"

Nick clicked to the next slide, to the graph that showed the five-year projections.

Sofia raised a brow. "Those numbers seem inflated."

"They're projections, sure, but I don't think they're inflated." He cut a glance to Lauren, who was also studying the screen. "My research team was very thorough."

Lauren's gaze connected with his for a second, then she looked back at the laptop.

Mrs. Ambrose said nothing, and as Nick wrapped up his presentation, he said, "Any questions about what I've shown you so far?"

Mrs. Ambrose leaned toward Sofia, and they whispered something together.

Then Sofia straightened. "Lauren mentioned that if we don't move forward with this partnership, then you'll sell your holdings in our company."

Nick refrained from looking at Lauren as he spoke. "I believe that Ambrose Oil is sitting on a gold mine, so to speak, and in my line of work, I invest in companies that are evolving with technology and focused on growth. I'd be remiss if I didn't tell you that I have other interests that I've considered moving my investments to. But Ambrose Oil's potential is too attractive for me to pursue other ventures if there's a chance that the three of you agree to sign off on a partnership."

Sofia's lips were pursed. Lauren shifted in her chair and folded her arms.

"Give us your terms, then, Mr. Matthews," Mrs. Ambrose said with a nod.

He met her gaze. "Fifty percent."

9

GETTING OFF THE plane in San Diego was a bit more simple than when Lauren had flown to Texas. First of all, she hadn't made a mistake in reserving a taxi, and there was no Nicholas Matthews to interfere with her life.

Well, he still wasn't completely out of the picture, but as far as Lauren was concerned, she'd never see him again. His offer of fifty percent had been ridiculous, outlandish, and insulting. Lauren's grandmother had immediately shut him down, and he'd had the gall to offer forty-eight percent instead. All of those adjectives she'd conjured up about him were only the beginning of what she thought of Nick.

Yeah, *Nick.* She was thinking of him as Nick and remembering how he'd shown up at the estate home half-wet. A good look on him, not that she'd admit that to anyone.

After Nicholas had finished his failed negotiation and Shelton had driven him back to wherever he'd been staying, Sofia had cornered Lauren.

"You're in trouble," Sofia had said. "You couldn't keep your eyes off him."

Lauren had laughed it off, but Sofia had looked far from convinced.

And now, Lauren could breathe easy, at least about Nick Matthews. She just hoped that he wouldn't pull his funding from Ambrose Oil.

As she climbed into the Lyft she'd scheduled, she checked her incoming emails and texts that she'd missed while on the plane. Sofia had texted: *So are you going to see Nicholas Matthews in San Diego? Don't you think it's a coincidence that you both live in the same city?*

Lauren grimaced as she texted back. *A lot of people live in San Diego. It's not like I'll see him at the coffee shop or anything.*

Sofia wrote back seconds later: *Fate is a funny thing.*

Now Lauren was annoyed. *This isn't fate. It was a business deal that's no longer a deal.*

You know Granny, Sofia wrote. *She says no to every venture capitalist. But I think Nick is different.*

This made Lauren both nervous and curious. *How so?*

The three dots on the texting app danced for longer than Lauren liked. Then Sofia's reply came. *I think he's going to adjust his offer. I think he's willing to negotiate. Did you see how he looked at you . . . it was like he couldn't keep his eyes off you. He's going to cave to Granny's demands.*

Lauren read the text twice, then a third time. She scoffed. *I don't believe it. He's no different than any other money-grubbing investor with a greed for oil and more oil.*

There. That should quiet her sister.

But Sofia wasn't done and had to have the last word. *I still think you're in trouble.*

Lauren shook her head and opened up her email app. She refused to entertain Sofia's suggestion that Nicholas Matthews was someone interested in her . . . he was interested in what Ambrose Oil could do to *his* bank account.

She had a handful of emails from charity organizations, most of which she was a regular sponsor of. The next email was from Freddie—the owner of the gallery. They'd sold another painting, which was always good news. Her art style wasn't for everyone. She mostly painted miniatures reminiscent of the Regency era, but her paintings were not always of people but of two disconnected subjects. Like a blue jay in the middle of a lake. The gallery owner had sent a reminder email about coming to the opening of another artist's display in order to drive traffic to the new artist. She'd almost forgotten about it.

Typically, Lauren didn't mind helping promote other artists, but the event was tonight, and she was looking forward to shutting the world out with a long bubble bath and the latest bestseller on her Kindle.

So instead of having a relaxing evening, Lauren took a quick shower, then changed into a mid-thigh black dress. It was her most formal and conservative dress, and she always wore it to gallery events. Then she arranged her hair into a twist and added some silver hoop earrings. She tucked the pendant of her necklace beneath her bodice edge.

Her grandmother had given her the pendant on her sixteenth birthday, calling it the Pendant of Protection. The pendant was in the shape of a heart, and on the back the inscription read *Together We Are Strong*. And none of the Ambrose women went without their good luck charm. Although Lauren didn't feel like luck was her friend right now.

Last, she slipped on strappy black sandals, then headed into the small kitchen of her condo to fetch her bag and cell phone.

She had two missed calls. One from Freddie and the second from Kevin.

She opened her voicemail and listened to the message from Freddie. Kevin hadn't left a message, and it was time to block him. She opened her settings and blocked the number, feeling better, but she hoped that would be the end of it. He knew where she lived, and she really didn't want to have to deal with calling the cops on him.

Lauren locked up her condo and headed to her car. The drive only took about twenty minutes, but the weather was perfect, and the mild warmth helped to relax her further. It was good to be back in San Diego, where she lived a relatively quiet life.

By the time she parked across the street from the gallery, there was a small crowd waiting on the sidewalk. Lauren was surprised to see so many people, especially for a newer artist. She crossed the street and headed around to the back entrance. Freddie looked up as she came through the back room. "Wonderful, you're here!"

"Did you doubt me?" she teased.

He strode to her, his tuxedo pristine, and kissed her cheek.

Stationed around the room were various white stands with sculptures on them by the artist Viola Jenns. The sculptures appeared to be abstract depictions of humans in various poses. The walls were adorned with miniatures by Lauren. "Where's Viola?" Lauren asked.

"She's, uh, in the powder room," Freddie said, fidgeting with his shirt cuffs. "She's been in there for ages. Could you be a sweetheart and ask if she's almost finished?" He glanced at the door. "I need to let them in soon."

"Nice that you have a crowd already," Lauren said.

"I think that's just her family," Freddie said in a lower voice. "She said all her cousins were coming."

Lauren glanced over the waiting group. She'd never met Viola, but now Lauren realized that most of the waiting people had red hair. What were the chances that Viola did too? "I'll go check on her."

Lauren walked to the bathroom, where the stenciled lettering on the door read *Ladies' Powder Room*. She pushed open the swinging door and stopped.

A red-headed woman leaned against the edge of the sink, wiping at tears streaking her face. She looked up at Lauren, and her blotchy face paled.

"Are you all right?" Lauren asked, coming the rest of the way into the bathroom.

"Oh," Viola said. "I'm not feeling well, and I . . ." She placed a hand to her chest. "I think something's wrong. I can't catch a full breath."

Lauren moved to the woman's side. "When did you start feeling this way?"

"On my way over here," Viola said in a small voice. She dabbed at her cheeks. "I thought maybe it was something I ate, you know, heartburn."

"Is this your first gallery showing?"

Viola nodded, her eyes filling with what looked like panic.

"I think you're just nervous," Lauren said. "Happens to all of us."

"You too?"

"Me too," Lauren said with a smile. "Do you know there's a bunch of people waiting outside to get in?"

Viola visibly swallowed. "Yeah, it's my family."

"That's amazing," Lauren said. "They must be so proud of you."

Viola nodded. "They are," she said in a whisper.

"Well . . ." Lauren rubbed Viola's shoulder. "How about we go out together? Freddie can let everyone in, and we'll celebrate your amazing work."

Viola's eyes widened. "You think it's amazing?"

"I do." Lauren squeezed the woman's shoulder. "Come on, let's go get them."

Viola turned to the mirror and groaned. "Everyone will know I've been crying."

"Here," Lauren said, opening her bag. "I've got some powder cover-up." She produced the compact and handed it over to Viola.

She quickly dusted her face, then said, "Okay, that's better."

Lauren smiled. "No one will know the difference."

"Thank you," Viola said.

"No problem." Lauren followed the woman into the gallery, then stood back as Viola greeted the slew of family members.

Freddie sidled up to Lauren. "Thank you for your help."

"You're welcome," Lauren said. "You know you can talk me into pretty much anything."

Freddie grinned. "I wish. I'd have you here every weekend helping out."

"I think her work will sell itself," Lauren said.

"Yeah, but I've had more than one person call to confirm that you would be here tonight."

Normally Lauren would be flattered, but after the attention from Kevin, she only felt worry. "Who?"

Freddie frowned. "I didn't get any names, if that's what you're wondering."

Lauren tried to not let it bother her. She was just being paranoid, and it wasn't like Kevin would show up someplace public like the gallery. She gave a brief smile to Freddie and moved over to the table with refreshments.

On her way, a couple of people stopped her and asked about her miniatures. For the next hour she talked to people, smiled, and answered questions, then encouraged them to look at Viola's work. Freddie, who was always discreet, took patrons to his desk and wrote up orders. He even sold a few of her miniatures, which was fine with Lauren.

About an hour into the event, Lauren saw a man walk in to the gallery, and for a second he reminded her of Nicholas Matthews. But that was impossible, she decided. He was too quickly swallowed up in the crowd, and Lauren didn't have a good view of him anyway from her position where she had been talking to a couple of college kids. Art majors.

"Lauren," a voice said.

She turned to see Viola with a woman who looked like an older version of her.

"This is my mom," Viola continued. "She wanted to meet you."

Viola's mom's smile was huge, and she grasped Lauren's hand. "I love your work," she gushed.

"Thank you," Lauren said, keeping a smile on her face. The woman seemed sincere, but in truth Lauren was counting down to the end of the evening. Maybe Freddie wouldn't mind if she skipped out a little early. Her feet were starting to ache, and that bubble bath was calling her name.

"Which one is your favorite miniature?" Viola's mom asked.

Lauren couldn't exactly turn down that question, so she led the woman to the wall of miniatures near the front of the gallery. Having such a large crowd was really nice, and Lauren was very happy for Viola's first showing.

As they stood in front of the wall, Lauren explained some of the miniatures to Viola's mother. She felt her excitement grow . . . this happened whenever she had a chance to talk in depth about her work. It also gave her more ideas, and Lauren realized she may not be sleeping so soon tonight after all.

Eventually, Viola's mother wandered away, and Lauren answered more questions from those who approached. Freddie came over more than once to put a *sold* notice on a miniature.

"Impressive," said a man to her left.

His voice was familiar, and even as she turned to see who'd spoken, she knew who he was.

Nicholas Matthews stood there, wearing a suit of course, his hands in his pockets.

"Nick?" she said.

The edges of his mouth lifted, and his hazel eyes locked with hers. "Hello, Lauren."

She could hardly believe he stood a few feet away from her . . . at the gallery in San Diego. She knew he lived in San Diego, of course, but what was he doing *here*? There was no way Sofia had been right. Not even her sister could have predicted this. Lauren could only guess that he wanted to talk to her about getting her grandmother to agree to the ridiculous forty-eight percent partnership offer.

Nick turned from her and lifted his chin to study the paintings on the wall. "These all yours?"

She should probably stop staring at his profile. "Yes." She blinked and looked at the painting he was currently studying.

"I didn't know dogs rode on trains," he said.

"Some do." She could smell that expensive cologne of his. All musky and male with a hint of pine.

"Do you have a dog?" he continued, as if it weren't extraordinary that they should be standing here, in the middle of this gallery, chatting.

"I don't have pets," she said. "But there's a cat who has claimed me as its official provider. Showed up one day, and I've been feeding it ever since."

He looked down at her and smiled.

Breathe. Lauren's mind raced with something to say, despite all the questions that were building up. "Do you have a pet, Nick?"

His smile faded, and he lifted a hand to rub the back of his neck. "I did. A dog."

She waited.

"He died last year."

Lauren knew he'd also lost his father last year. Must have been a rough time. "Sorry. What was his name?"

"Her name was Lady, or Little Lady."

Lauren liked the softness she saw in Nick's eyes. Not that she was going to change her mind about him, but it was good to see that he had some human component to him. "As in *Lady and the Tramp*?"

He chuckled, and Lauren wasn't sure if she'd heard him laugh before.

"I'm not going to answer that," he said. "Sometimes pets decide on their own name, you know?"

"I do know," Lauren said. "Like the cat I feed told me her name was Silver."

Nick's brows shot up. "Really. Let me guess, does she have gray fur?"

"She prefers to call it silver," Lauren said.

His smile was warm. "And does Silver ride trains?"

"I have no idea," she said. "But there's a lot I still don't know about her."

Nick nodded, his eyes filled with amusement. "Cats can be like that. My mother has one."

The crowd jostled around them, and someone bumped into Lauren. She stepped sideways to keep her balance, which meant she bumped into Nick. He grasped her arm to steady her.

"Sorry," she said.

"No problem."

He was still holding her arm.

"So what brings you here tonight?" Lauren said, folding her arms, which caused Nick to drop his hand. She didn't let herself think about his smooth, warm fingers.

"I was thinking how we got off on the wrong foot in Ambrose," he said in a low voice. "And I wanted to rectify that."

Oh, this was rich. "And how did you intend to do that?"

"Well," he said, slipping his hands into his pockets again. "I was thinking that we could go out for dinner after you've finished up here."

10

NICK WONDERED IF he'd ever seen a woman look more surprised at his invitation to dinner. But Lauren Ambrose topped them all. Was it really so shocking? Yeah, it probably was. He wasn't exactly on her friend list or even on her respected business associate list. Somehow they'd ended up talking about cats, though, so maybe there was some hope of continued civility between them.

"Why?" she said, her tone changing from the soft, almost flirty tone from moments before to suspicious. "So you can try to talk me into changing my grandmother's mind?"

Nick opened his mouth, then closed it again. "No business. Just . . . an apology." Maybe this hadn't been such a good idea after all.

The suspicion didn't leave her expression. "Look, thanks for coming to the gallery, and I wish you all the best with everything, but—"

"One hour," he said. "That's all." Why was he pushing this? And why had he come at all? It was like she had cast some sort of spell over him and he hadn't been able to stop thinking about her since . . . well, since he met her at the airport.

It was probably the first time in his adult life that he didn't have an end goal in mind. He'd shown up, seen her in her fitted black dress, those blue eyes with the depths of a vast pool, her bare pink lips . . . and he wanted to talk to her. Stand closer to her. See if she still smelled like wildflowers and honey. He could now confirm that was the case.

"I don't think so, Nick," she said, but her tone was less wary now. Almost . . . like she wanted him to convince her.

"There's an Italian place two blocks from here," he said. "We could walk if you wanted. I know the manager, and they'll get us right in. The shrimp scampi is amazing. Completely authentic."

"And you would know," she said, her gaze scanning him, until her eyes reached his shoes.

He smiled. "My favorite place to buy shoes."

Her gaze returned to his face. "Do you go to Italy a lot?"

"A few times a year." He moved slightly closer. "Have you been?"

"No."

He was openly staring at her, that he knew, but it seemed he couldn't do anything about it. "You should come with me." He had no idea where that had come from, but he couldn't take it back now.

Lauren laughed, which sent all kinds of relief through him. She thought he was joking, and yeah, he was, sort of. Impulsiveness was not his norm, and tonight had been completely impulsive.

She patted his chest, and it took everything he could do not to grasp her hand and hold it there. All too soon, she'd lowered her hand. "I wouldn't want to cramp your style, Mr. CEO."

His brows lifted. "What style are you referring to, Ms. Ambrose?"

Her lips parted, and his heart rate moved up a notch because he was thinking about things he shouldn't be.

"Oh, you know, the man who has everything," she said, her lips curving into a smile. "Money, looks, charm—"

"Wait, what about my looks?" he asked.

Her smile widened, and her cheeks stained pink. "Your head's big enough, sir. I wouldn't want it to explode." She moved a step away from him. "I've got a really busy night, and so I won't be able to go to dinner. Thanks for the invitation, though."

Nick grasped her hand before she could turn away. She stilled, then looked over her shoulder. She didn't pull her hand from his, even though he held it loosely.

"One hour," he said. "Everyone needs to eat, including you."

She bit her lip, and he could see the indecision in those blue eyes of hers.

"One hour, two blocks," he tried again. He dropped her hand and stepped back. "I'll wait outside in case you change your mind."

He turned then and wove his way through the crowd. He could feel her gaze on his back. Good. She was thinking about it. Meanwhile, he'd continue his streak of impulsivity and wait outside the gallery like some Romeo trying to get attention from his Juliet.

It turned out that he didn't have to wait long. Only about fifteen minutes—well, fourteen minutes to be exact. When she stepped out of the gallery, her bag over her shoulder, the tension eased from his shoulders.

Beneath the moonlight, she looked different, more fragile, more ethereal. But he knew she was far from fragile.

"Is it really two blocks?" she asked.

Nick straightened from where he'd been leaning against the building. "I can pull it up on my phone and show you."

The edges of her mouth lifted as she studied him.

Nick strode toward her, joining her in the light spilling out from the gallery windows. His heart might be thumping in anticipation, but he kept his voice neutral. "Do you want to walk?" He couldn't stop his gaze from sliding to her heeled sandals.

She folded her arms, that smile still playing on her lips. "Where's your car?"

This was more than what he'd expected. "Around the corner," he gestured behind him, "the opposite way of the restaurant."

She shrugged and moved past him, walking in the direction he'd pointed. "I've been standing in these heels for two hours, so we might as well drive."

Nick was at her side in an instant. They didn't talk as they walked to the corner.

A car passed, then another. The second one slowed down and angled toward the red-painted curb.

A man jumped out of the car, and Nick paused, wondering if he needed help.

Lauren came to a complete stop.

"Lauren!" the man said. "Are you leaving already?"

"Kevin?" she said in a faint voice.

Nick looked from Lauren to the man who'd illegally parked and was now approaching them. Wasn't this the guy she said was her ex-boyfriend? Maybe they'd gotten back together?

Lauren moved closer to Nick and slipped her arm through his. Nick truly didn't mind, but he wasn't sure it was for the reason he was hoping.

Kevin was only a few feet away now, and the streetlamp illuminated his distressed face.

"I had to see you," Kevin said. "You blocked my number."

"We broke up, remember," Lauren said in an even tone, although her grip tightened on Nick's arm.

Kevin's gaze slid to Nick. "You cheated on me with this guy?"

"What I do is no longer your business," Lauren said. "You need to leave now, or I'll call the police."

Kevin's eyes bugged out. "Really? You're seriously whacked—"

Nick stepped forward, moving in front of Lauren. "She asked you to *leave*, Kevin."

"This is between us," Kevin spat out. "Move out of my way."

The second Kevin tried to shove Nick, he was ready. Nick grabbed the guy's shirt and hauled him close, stopping within inches of his face. Nick had him in both height and weight, and Kevin knew it.

"You can leave in peace," Nick ground out, "or I can make you leave."

Kevin stared at Nick, and he could see the debate in the guy's eyes. "Don't be stupid," Nick said in a low voice. "Stalking a woman is a crime."

"I'm not . . ." His voice trailed off as a police siren sounded in the distance. No one had called the police, but it was enough to alert Kevin.

"I'm going now," Kevin said, pulling away from Nick.

Nick held on for another second, just to show that he could, then he released Kevin.

He stumbled back, then turned and hurried back to his car.

Nick stood on the sidewalk, his arms folded, as he watched Kevin do a lousy three-point turn to get his car going in the right direction.

After he sped off down the road and disappeared around a corner, Nick faced Lauren.

She was standing still, one hand on her mouth, her eyes wide.

"Are you okay?" he asked.

She lowered her hand and nodded. Then she shook her head. "I can't believe he did that. I mean, I didn't think he was that type."

"Well, he's that type," Nick said. "What else has he done?"

Lauren looked away. "Just phone calls, but I blocked his number today, and . . ." She wiped at her face.

Nick hated that she was crying over this jerk. "Hey." He touched her arm gently. "We don't have to go out. I was just—"

She stepped closer and wrapped her arms about his waist, stunning Nick. He pulled her close. He couldn't tell if she was crying, but if she needed comfort, he was only too happy to give it.

A couple of cars passed by them on the street, and each time Lauren tensed.

"Does he know where you live?"

She nodded against his chest.

"Do you want to file a report at the police station?" he asked, rubbing a slow circle on her back.

"No," she said. "I think you scared him off. And it might be good for him to think you and I are . . . together. Cut through whatever overzealous thoughts he might have about me."

Nick frowned, not entirely convinced at her line of reasoning. He assumed she lived alone, and that would put her at risk. "Do you need a place to stay for a while?"

She looked up at him. "I'll be fine. I was just taken off guard." She drew away from him, and Nick caught her hand.

"Are you sure?"

She nodded. At least she wasn't crying anymore, and that was good, but still, Nick's stomach felt like it had been hollowed out.

"I'm starving," she said.

"Well, I think we could fix that."

A small smile touched her lips, and he wanted to pull her close again.

"Okay, but you have to do one thing first."

At that moment, he realized he'd pretty much do anything she asked of him. "Name it."

This time she gave him a real smile. Then she reached up and unknotted his tie.

He found he was holding his breath for some ridiculous reason, but the brush of her fingertips against his neck sent a warm buzz through him. She slid off his tie, then rolled it up and put it into that multicolored bag of hers that seemed to hold a plethora of mysterious items.

But she wasn't done yet apparently.

Lauren grasped the edges of his lapels and tugged his suit jacket over both shoulders. He shrugged out of it, helping her along, because he was helpful that way.

"Much better." Her eyes gleamed with amusement. "I feel like walking after all." She draped the jacket over her arm, then turned from him, heading down the street. "Coming?" she asked, glancing over her shoulder.

He'd been staring. "Yeah." He forced himself to walk, feeling strangely exhilarated at her actions and the way he had enjoyed her taking the initiative in their relationship. That thought gave him pause. Relationship?

He was really glad that Lauren Ambrose couldn't read minds.

11

THE RESTAURANT WAS cozy, beautiful, and smelled totally authentic. Or at least how Lauren imagined a restaurant would smell in Italy. When the waitress set down a basket of fresh, hot bread, Lauren felt the knots in her stomach begin to loosen. Nick had led her into the restaurant, his hand at the small of her back, as more than one person greeted him.

He hadn't been kidding; he was a regular here.

Their booth was tucked away in the far corner of the restaurant, and the velvet seat coverings and the three candles on the table made Lauren feel like she was in a 1930s movie. Lauren decided right then and there that she wouldn't tell Sofia about this little outing. Lauren could just imagine Sofia's I-told-you-so attitude, which would not be helpful at all. No, this would stay Lauren's own business.

"May I take your drink orders?" The waitress appeared, her jet-black hair smoothed into a twist and her dark-red lipstick setting off her olive skin. "The usual for you, Nick?"

Nick smiled at the woman. "Yes, thanks."

Her name badge read *Francesca*.

Lauren tried not to feel the envy that was warming up her chest. Francesca was beautiful, and she obviously knew Nick—beyond the restaurant? Lauren had no idea, and it wasn't any of her concern, but she was definitely curious.

Francesca turned her sultry gaze upon Lauren. "What will you have, ma'am?"

Lauren ordered hot tea. Ever since Kevin's unexpected visit, her goose bumps wouldn't go away.

When Francesca left, Lauren watched her walk away, marveling at how effortlessly the waitress moved about the restaurant in stilettos.

Lauren felt Nick's studied gaze on her, and she looked over at him.

"Are you dating her?" Might as well get it all out in the open.

Nick blinked. "Francesca? Uh, no."

"She was giving you that look."

"What look?" Nick rested his forearms on the table.

Lauren waved her hand. "You know, that look women give men when they want something."

His mouth quirked, and his hazel eyes scanned her face. "Care to demonstrate?"

"No," she said. "I could never compare to an Italian woman."

Nick didn't say anything for a moment, and just as Lauren was thinking about picking up her menu, he said, "What if it's the other way around?"

"What?" Lauren said.

"That Francesca could never compare to *you*," he said in a quiet tone.

Lauren probably didn't need the hot tea now; she was plenty warm. "I'm not naïve," she said, "and I'm pretty sure you're not either."

"You're right, I'm not naïve," he said, but he was gazing at her with a thoughtful expression, and Lauren didn't know how to read it.

"Thanks for your help, uh, back there with Kevin."

He nodded, but his gaze was sharp. "I don't like that he found you so easily. He could come to your place too."

Lauren had to look away. It had been her exact worry.

"Look, Lauren," he said in a careful tone. "I have a two-level house on the beach. You could stay on one level. You know, until you think that Kevin has given up."

Lauren met his gaze again. She could see the sincerity in his eyes and hear it in his voice. But it was going too far . . . "I'll be okay, really."

Nick didn't seem surprised at her answer. He picked up his phone. "Let's swap numbers, and then if you change your mind—"

"Here's that water, Mr. Matthews," Francesca said, arriving at their table.

She might have called Nick by Mr. Matthews, but on Francesca's lips, it sounded intimate.

So maybe he really did order water all of the time if it was his usual at this restaurant. "And your tea," Francesca continued, setting down a saucer and tea cup. She added a platter of tea condiments.

"Have you decided on your meals yet?" Francesca's dark gaze was back on Nick. "The usual?"

"That sounds good," he said.

"I'll have what he's having," Lauren said. It was the quickest way to get rid of the waitress and all of those suggestive looks she kept giving Nick. If they really hadn't dated, Lauren was pretty sure that Francesca wished they had.

When she walked away, Nick looked at Lauren with amusement. "You don't even know what I ordered."

"Well, if you like it, then I should too." Or, more accurately, she'd ordered the same thing as Nick for Francesca's benefit.

"That sounds perfectly logical," Nick said, his smile growing.

Lauren hid a sigh. He really had a beautiful smile.

"I like you, Lauren Ambrose."

She laughed. He wasn't saying he *liked* her but that he liked her bantering.

Then his expression sobered. "Think about my offer. I don't want Kevin to think he can bother you again."

"I'll be fine, truly," she said. "I've lived alone my entire adult life."

He said nothing for a second, just studied her. "At least give me your number, and vice versa. You can call me if anything changes."

That sounded reasonable. She picked up her bag and dug her phone out of it, then said in a low, sultry tone to match Francesca's, "What's your number, Mr. Matthews?"

He chuckled and slid her phone from her grasp. He added his number, then handed the phone over. "Call me so I have yours."

Lauren looked down at the contact he'd created. It was simply *Nick*. No *Nicholas Matthews* or *Nick Matthews*.

"Okay." She pressed the call button.

His phone buzzed, then he created a contact from the number on his phone.

Unexpectedly, Lauren felt comfort in knowing that she had his number, and he had hers . . . if only because of Kevin. Not that she thought he'd continue to cause problems, but it was nice to know she could call Nick.

It wasn't like she'd call Sofia—who was a couple of states away. She couldn't do anything.

"How long have you been painting?" Nick asked after drinking some of his water.

"Since high school, I guess," Lauren said, then she tried her tea. "I found out that I loved it in one of those mandatory art classes."

Nick clasped his hands together. "So, why miniatures?"

It was a good question. "I guess I thought it was interesting to see how much I could get into such a small space. It's not the best art, I know."

"It's great art," Nick countered. "And you're very talented."

Lauren had been complimented plenty of times on her work, so why did Nick's compliment make her face warm? "Thanks, but you don't need to build up my confidence. I don't need a regular job like most people, so I'm lucky to do something I love. Believe me, I know how unique that is."

Nick's hazel eyes didn't leave her face. "I'm not trying to build up your confidence. I like your art, plain and simple. In fact, I bought a couple of pieces tonight."

She stared at him. "You . . . did?" She swallowed, suddenly feeling like she should apologize or something. Tell him that he was under no obligation. Then her gaze narrowed. "Are you brown-nosing?"

He chuckled, and Lauren hated that his laugh warmed her through. Either that, or her tea was doing its job.

"I'm not brown-nosing."

Lauren didn't believe him for a minute. "Then wining and dining," she said.

"I don't see wine, do you?" He was still smiling. "We could order some if that would make you feel better."

She shook her head. "I think I need to keep my head on straight around you in case you try to use your powers of persuasion."

Nick leaned forward, his gaze intently interested. "What do you think I'm trying to persuade you to do?"

"Not to *do*, specifically, but to believe."

His brows raised. "Care to elaborate?"

"Not really." Lauren exhaled. "You said this wasn't a business dinner."

"It's not," he said. "But we could talk about business if you want to. Although . . ." He took another sip of his water. "I'd rather not."

His intense gaze on her, the quiet music, the candles glowing on the table, his close proximity, which meant she could smell his cologne . . . all of that was messing with her mind. This man was incredibly good-looking, and he knew it. He probably had a dozen Francescas saved in his phone.

"Fair enough," Lauren said. "So tell me about yourself, Nicholas Matthews."

His expression held amusement. "What do you want to know?"

"Well, what makes you tick?"

His chuckle was low. "Numbers."

She should have guessed it. He was a finance guy, after all. "Have you always loved numbers?"

"They're straightforward, and numbers never lie," he said. "I love it when they balance out."

"So you're an accountant at heart?"

"That's what I went to school for, and it wasn't until a few years ago when my dad pulled me into his company that I worked more with investments," Nick said. "I would have been perfectly happy running my own accounting firm, but working for my dad was unexpectedly enjoyable."

Lauren was impressed that Nick enjoyed working for his dad. Family businesses were tricky. "That sounds nice."

Nick shrugged. "We didn't always see eye to eye, but age matured me, and age mellowed my dad. Besides, there's not much travel in accounting. So traveling now has been an added perk."

She smirked. "You bought your shoes in Italy, didn't you?"

"Doesn't everyone?"

Lauren laughed. "No, we do not."

"So . . ." he prompted.

She met his gaze. "I don't travel much, okay? I'm perfectly happy with my San Diego condo, my work, and not having to be anyplace at a specific time."

Nick eyed her speculatively. "What's the farthest you've been?"

Lauren hesitated, not having admitted this to anyone. "Um . . . New York."

He blinked. "You've never been out of the country?"

She shook her head, feeling breathless for some reason.

He sat back, disbelief in his eyes, not that she exactly blamed him. "You're kidding," he said.

Now she was annoyed. This is why she usually kept private things about her life private. "I'm not kidding. I've been busy. It's hard to explain to someone who's not an artist. But when I'm painting, not much else matters. It's kind of like being in my own world, I guess."

He didn't answer for a moment. "When you studied art, didn't you want to go see the great works for yourself?"

Lauren's eyes burned for some reason. Yeah, she had. Dearly. But she hadn't wanted to go by herself. And to become good enough friends with someone in order to travel out of the country meant she'd have to do things that friends did. Talk about her past, who she really was—and she knew she was a juxtaposition.

Just then, the food arrived, and as Francesca set their platters before them, Lauren decided she was grateful for the interruption.

12

Nick unlocked the door to his home and stepped into the dark interior. The place smelled of cleaning solution, which told him that Mallory had been there to clean that day. He'd texted her not to prepare a meal since he'd hoped to convince Lauren to go out to eat with him.

He didn't know what had driven him to visit her at the gallery tonight. He'd wanted to see her, plain and simple. No real agenda. Yeah, the business deal with her grandmother had taken a detour, but in no way did Nick think it was a closed door.

Most business deals took detours until the terms were agreed upon. He believed that with a few weeks of patience on his part, Mrs. Lillian Ambrose and her granddaughters would see that the benefits were much stronger than the drawbacks.

But that wasn't why he'd gone to see Lauren. Maybe he was just curious to see her in her world of art and galleries and also to view her works up close.

He'd bought the two paintings with cats in them. The thought made him smile as he flipped on a light and headed into the vast gourmet kitchen. It had been one of the draws of the beach house when he'd been looking for a place in San Diego. After he joined his father's company, he'd moved down from Newport to be closer to company headquarters.

Nick opened the fridge and took out a water bottle. Dropping Lauren off at her car had been hard. He'd wanted to follow her to her condo, check the place out, make sure everything was secure. But she'd assured him that she had a great security system and that Kevin didn't have a key or any codes.

Still... Nick opened the water bottle and guzzled half of it down. He probably needed caffeine after the rich Italian meal in order to stay alert for his conference calls starting in about an hour. He'd be attending a board meeting, via videoconferencing, for one of his venture companies headquartered in London.

But if he had caffeine now, there was no way he'd be able to fall asleep in a few hours. Lauren was already plaguing his mind enough.

He picked up the suit jacket that she'd taken off, and he shrugged into it. She'd kept his tie and had probably forgotten about it by now. And he hadn't reminded her. So he headed into his bedroom and selected another tie, then slipped it around his collar and did up the knot.

Next, he headed down the hall, then turned into the office, where the floor-to-ceiling windows gave him a view of the Pacific. Without the lights on, the moon seemed to light up the whole expanse of the ocean.

He crossed to the windows and gazed out of them for several moments. Lauren's questions about his dad had stirred up all sorts of memories, from the early conversations with his dad about coming to work for Matthews Capital and Holdings. Nick's initial resistance. Then his dad's confession that he was having a heart stent put in that weekend.

The news had shaken up Nick's view of his successful and healthy father.

"I won't live forever," his dad said. "And although I'm not ready to kick the bucket yet, I'd rather leave Matthews Capital and Holdings in the hands of my very capable son instead of the board."

Nick had flown to San Diego for a few days for the surgery. His mom hadn't come, but there had been several phone conversations between his parents.

About two weeks after the surgery, his dad had brought up the subject again, this time in a rare conference call with both of his parents.

They both thought Nick was talented and ready. And the grooming began.

He finished off the water bottle, then tossed it into the trash next to the desk. He checked the time on his phone. He still had time to review the agenda he'd put together for the meeting. So he turned on the office lights and powered up his desktop.

By the time the meeting started, his mind had finally reverted to all things business. Any tiredness he'd felt was gone, and he was hyper-focused, drilling down through the agenda items. They were halfway through the agenda when his cell phone buzzed with a text. Nick glanced at the time and saw that it was one in the morning.

And the text was from Lauren.

Nick's breath stalled when he saw what she'd written.

Did you knock on my door a few minutes ago?

Nick felt frozen. He quickly texted her back: *No. Can you call me?*

Then he spoke into his headset. "I need a five-minute break." Without waiting for an answer from the board, he switched his screen, then texted a question mark to Lauren. He didn't even have her address, so how would he be at her place, knocking?

His phone rang seconds later, and she sounded out of breath.

"Hi, sorry to bother you," she said in a rush. "I think it was just teenagers goofing off. You know, door ditching."

Nick rose to his feet and paced to the windows. "Did you see them?"

"No, I mean, I was almost asleep when someone knocked, so by the time I got to the door, they were gone."

He exhaled. "Have you had door ditchers before at your complex?"

Her voice sounded faint when she replied, "Not exactly."

Nick closed his eyes. "Text me your address. I'm coming to pick you up."

"Nick, really, that's kind of extreme, don't you think?"

"I don't like the timing or the coincidence of what happened with Kevin tonight, do you?"

"Well, no—"

"Just send me your address," he said. "I'll check out the place, and then we can go from there. But I think you need to call your complex's security as well."

She hesitated, but then she said, "Okay."

When Nick hung up with Lauren, he returned to the board meeting. "Sorry, everyone, I have an emergency. Please continue with the agenda, and email me the decisions made. I'll go over them as soon as I can."

He clicked off again and headed to the kitchen to grab the key fob he'd left on the counter. Five minutes later, he was speeding along the dark streets of San Diego, heading in Lauren's direction. Frustration pounded through him. She should have come home with him in the first place. If Kevin was at her complex, he might not stop at door ditching.

Even now, he might be lurking, making plans.

Nick used his Bluetooth to call Lauren. He exhaled with relief when she answered.

"Is everything okay?" he asked.

"Yeah," she said. "I'm just putting together a few things for tonight."

"Where are you?"

She paused. "In my bedroom."

"Is everything locked in your place? Doors and windows?"

"Yeah, at least I think so . . ." Her voice trailed off. "Not sure about the kitchen window. I sometimes leave it open."

A shiver ran through him. "Does your bedroom door lock?"

"Yes."

"Lock it until I get there," he said. "And stay on the phone with me."

"Okay."

The tension in her voice was clear, and Nick wished he could speed through all the red lights. Each one seemed agonizingly slow. By the time he reached the complex, the urgency had only grown inside of him. He entered the gate code that Lauren had given him.

"Everything still okay?" he asked as he drove his car toward her building.

Even though he'd asked her that a dozen times, she said, "Yeah."

"Good," he murmured, then pulled into a stall and parked. Climbing out of the car, he glanced around, checking for moving shadows, an idling car, anything that might stand out this time of night. But all seemed quiet.

Nick wasn't fooled into relaxing, though. He strode to Lauren's door and texted: *I'm here.*

Moments later, the door cracked open.

"Hey," he said in a soft voice.

She opened the door wider, and he stepped across the threshold. A single light was on, keeping the room dim, and he scanned the room while she shut the door. She had several large watercolors on the wall, and he wondered if they were done by her. Their pastel colors were landscapes that looked similar to the property around Ambrose Estate.

When he turned back to face Lauren, she was leaning against the door, her eyes wide as if she was spooked.

"You okay?" he said, although he'd asked her more than a dozen times tonight.

She nodded, then bit her lip.

Next thing he knew, she'd closed the distance between them and slipped her arms about his waist.

"Thanks for coming," she whispered. "I was about to lose my mind."

He wrapped his arms about her shoulders, holding her close. "I'm glad you called."

She said nothing, only held onto him.

He lowered his chin, resting it on the top of her head. This was a new thing for him, to be holding a woman simply because he was grateful she was safe. The embrace somehow turned more intimate as he began to notice small things, like the scent of her hair, the warmth of her breath against his skin, the way her heart was racing . . .

"Let's get your things," he said in a quiet voice, easing her out of the embrace. He needed to cool off before he cradled her face and kissed those lips of hers.

Lauren blinked up at him as if she were coming out of a fog. Nick felt the same way. He smoothed some of her hair behind her ear, then let his fingers brush against her neck.

She stepped away then, and his hand dropped. "Give me a second." She moved past him and headed down the hallway.

Nick exhaled, refocused, and checked all of the windows in the kitchen and throughout the front room. By the time Lauren returned with her multicolored bag over one shoulder and a blue duffle bag in her other hand, Nick was thinking much more clearly.

"Does this place have security cameras?" he asked.

"Yeah," Lauren said. "Do you think they would have caught something?"

"It's worth finding out." Nick opened the front door. He took the duffle bag as Lauren stepped through the doorway. The weight of it surprised him. "What do you have in here?"

"Some art supplies," she said. "Don't worry, they're non-fragrant."

Nick wasn't worried, just curious.

He waited as Lauren locked the door, then he led the way to his sports car and opened the passenger door for her. Then he set the duffle in the trunk, and on his way to the driver's side, he glanced around again. Looking for any movement, any out-of-place shadow.

Seeing nothing, he joined Lauren in the car. And as they drove out of the complex, Nick couldn't quite explain the relief that pulsed through him, but he was glad that Lauren had agreed to come with him.

13

THE SUNLIGHT STREAMED across the guest bedroom, where Lauren had spent the night. She guessed it to be almost noon by the warmth and intensity of the brightness. Turning over, she grabbed her cell from the nightstand. Sure enough, it was twelve thirty. She hoped that Nick wouldn't be annoyed that she'd slept so long, but in truth, she hadn't gone to bed until about six that morning.

After Nick had given her a tour of the beach house, she'd been too keyed up to sleep. So she'd started a new miniature painting, and the hours slid by. She had no idea how long Nick had stayed up, because he'd gone downstairs to the main part of the beach house. He'd told her that he had some work to do, but whenever she got up in the morning to help herself to whatever was in the kitchen.

Lauren pulled the coverlet higher and burrowed into the downy softness. The guest room was on the top floor of the gorgeous beach house, and the view was stunning from the floor-to-ceiling windows. She could easily stay in bed for another hour and just watch the undulating waves of the Pacific.

Was Nick even home? He'd mentioned an office downtown and that he'd been on a conference call with a London client when she'd texted him. So where was he now? No sounds reached her, and the silence only made her curious. She climbed out of bed, changed from her PJ shorts and tank top, and pulled on yoga pants and a T-shirt. Then she smoothed her hair into a ponytail.

Picking up her phone, she debated whether or not to tell Sofia that she was staying at Nick's house. No . . . there was nothing going on. There was no reason to create any family drama. As far as Lauren was concerned, if Nick did present a counteroffer, it would have nothing to do with her.

She left the guest bedroom and walked barefoot down the stairs to the main floor. In the daylight, the place was even more gorgeous. Pale-gray walls followed the arc of giant windows, overlooking the beach and ocean beyond. All the furniture was square and pale gray or white, but it looked comfortable enough. She padded into the pristine kitchen that had all the implements of a professional gourmet kitchen.

"Nick?" she called, just to cover her bases. No answer. She wasn't going to text him and bother him if he really was at his downtown office.

She crossed to the fridge and opened it. Several containers of food graced the shelves, all of them labeled in a decidedly feminine hand. Lauren pulled out a container of cut-up fruit. She found a fork and ate a few pieces.

As she ate, she heard a faint thumping. Like a soft, rhythmic thud. Maybe she *wasn't* alone. She listened for a moment, then walked around the kitchen island and headed down a hallway toward the sound. The thudding grew louder, and at the end of the hallway, a door sat partially open. At first glance, Lauren realized it was a workout room.

She moved a step closer and caught a glimpse of Nick running on a treadmill. He was wearing wireless earbuds and seemed oblivious to her presence. He wore athletic shorts and running shoes, and that was it. No shirt. Lauren really shouldn't be spying on him, but she'd never seen Nick so . . . undressed before.

She had the perfect view of his back, as he faced the long windows overlooking the beach. And the mirrors on the side of the room gave her a peek at his torso. His sculpted physique made it pretty obvious that he never skipped a day working out in some fashion. She was pretty sure he was in the 2 percent fat bracket.

Lauren swallowed. She'd already determined he was a beautiful man, but Nick without a shirt was something to behold. And now she felt all kinds of warm, which meant she should return to the kitchen immediately.

Then he turned his head, and their eyes connected through the mirror. His step faltered on the treadmill, and Lauren jerked back into the hallway, her breath suddenly gone.

He'd seen her staring at him. Sure enough, the treadmill powered off, and there were no more thudding footsteps.

"Lauren?" His deep voice cut through her embarrassment.

"Yeah?" she said, keeping to the hallway. No doubt her face had flamed red.

And then he came out into the hall, using a hand towel to wipe his neck. In his other hand, he carried a water bottle. "Sorry, I didn't hear you. Did I wake you up?"

Lauren wanted to look everywhere but at him. The sheen of perspiration that covered his face and neck and shoulders and chest, and lower . . . it should have been a turnoff, because he was a sweaty man, right? But warmth pooled in her belly at the sight. The scent of expensive cologne was gone, replaced by perspiration and spice, a combination that didn't bother her at all.

"Um, no," she said. "I heard thumping when I went into the kitchen, and I thought I'd investigate. I didn't know if you were here or at your downtown office." His breathing was starting to slow down, and Lauren stole a glance at him, then dutifully looked away again.

He took a drink from the water bottle, and Lauren was sure to keep her gaze averted.

"Lauren, I wasn't about to leave you alone," he said. "Not after a night like last night."

She nodded. He was being way too courteous. "You could have gone into your office . . . I'm fine."

She felt his gaze on her.

"Did you sleep okay?" he asked.

"Um, yeah, once I fell asleep," she said, glancing at him again. "I painted for a while."

"Is that what you were doing with the light on?" he said, studying her. "I didn't know if you sleep with the light on or if you were spooked or something."

"I sleep with the light off," she said in a quiet voice. "Were you checking on me?"

"I didn't want to disturb you, but I might have gone upstairs a time or two."

Lauren was warm again. Would it be rude to snatch his water bottle and drink it down? "Well, I'm fine, and thanks for your help. But I should get out of your way now." She waved a hand at his body. "You're busy, and I . . ." Her gaze involuntarily moved down the length of his body. "I have stuff to do."

Nick smiled when their eyes connected again.

Oh dear. Could she be any more obvious?

"Like what?" he asked.

"Like . . . stuff. Lots of stuff." She turned. "I'll clean up the food in the kitchen, then get my things. Don't worry about driving me, I'll call a Lyft."

She didn't even get three steps down the hall before Nick grasped her arm.

"Lauren, wait," he said in a quiet voice.

Slowly, she turned to face him. He dropped his hand. "Stay, for breakfast or lunch or whatever. We need to get that security footage before you return to your place. I talked to one of my lawyers this morning, and he recommended that you file a protective order against Kevin. It holds more weight than a restraining order."

Lauren blinked. In truth, she wasn't planning on going back to her place tonight. She'd check into a hotel for a few nights, because, yeah, she was nervous. Staying here would be really nice, but she could barely keep her eyes off of Nick and her mind focused when she was around him. A hotel was the safer option.

"I can't put you out," Lauren said. "I mean, you've been more than generous, but you have a life, and it's pretty much against everything in my personality to rely on someone else."

"Really?" Nick said, sounding intrigued. "Is that why you live in a tiny condo in a questionable neighborhood?"

"It's not that bad."

The edges of Nick's mouth lifted, and he moved closer to her. "You can stay here; there's plenty of room."

Lauren took a step back because his presence was filling up the entire hallway. "I really hate to be in anyone's way. For all I knew, the thudding was because you had a special guest over and you were engaged in a vigorous activity." The second the words left her mouth, she could have kicked herself.

Nick's eyes widened, then he laughed. "You're funny, Lauren Ambrose."

She stepped back again, mortification pounding through her. "I'm sorry," she whispered. "I didn't mean . . . I didn't think."

He shook his head slowly, but amusement filled his eyes. "So you came down the hall to investigate?"

She wanted to disappear. "No." She bit her lip and looked away.

Nick chuckled and moved closer still. She was next to the wall, and he braced a hand against the wall, only a few inches from her head. She didn't move, couldn't have moved if she tried. His hazel eyes were focused on her with an intensity that made her skin buzz. "Believe me, the last thing I'd do is have a special guest over when the beautiful Lauren Ambrose is sleeping in my house."

Her throat went dry. She wanted to look away from him, push off the wall, and head to the kitchen. Instead, she stared into his eyes. His gaze slipped to her mouth, and her heart about pounded out of her chest.

What was happening? Was she being completely duped so that she'd talk her grandma into taking his company's offer? Or was she just weak-kneed at the sight of a handsome man wearing no shirt?

She pressed a single finger against his warm chest. "You're sweaty, and I have things to do."

Nick smiled. "All that stuff?"

"Yeah, lots of stuff." She slid past him, and as she headed toward the kitchen she felt his gaze on her every step of the way.

Once in the kitchen, she took another bite of the cantaloupe, then she put the container away. The thudding started up again, and it reminded Lauren of what she'd said to him. Face heating again, she got herself a glass of ice water. With double the ice.

14

NICK MISSED HER.

Lauren had been back in her place for a week now, and he didn't like it. For three nights she'd stayed with him, and although the protective order had been filed and the security cameras at her complex inconclusive about who'd door-ditched her, Nick still didn't like her on her own.

But Lauren Ambrose was one stubborn woman, and he knew where she got it from.

Lillian and Sofia Ambrose had sent back some changes to the contract he'd offered them. This was a huge step in the right direction, and although he wouldn't be able to meet most of their demands, at least they were making them. He considered this a positive step, because it told him that the deal was getting real.

And he was pretty sure Lauren didn't know about the negotiating. He guessed that she'd be caught up soon enough; after all, she'd have to vote on any major change in the company, and this would be a significant contract.

The conference call he was now on was going longer than he'd planned. He'd already presented his ideas, and now the other three executives of the small plane company were going over each point thoroughly. Nick's administrative assistant, Paulie, was taking notes on her iPad as she sat across the wide conference table from him. Paulie wore her green-rimmed glasses today, which matched her green hoop earrings and green-striped shirt. The fifty-something woman had her own style, and that was one of the things Nick liked about her. That and her no-nonsense personality.

He fiddled with his phone, still paying attention while he scrolled through the texts between him and Lauren over the past week. Mostly him asking, "How are you doing?" And her saying, "Good."

Lauren wasn't much of a texter. And she'd only answered once when he'd called. It was driving him crazy. *She* was driving him crazy. Even with her one-word texts, he could hear her voice in them. And if he closed his eyes, he could see her in his mind. The first time at the airport curb with her wild hair. At her grandmother's estate, wearing that navy dress. At the gallery in those black heels. Then, at his home, her messy bun, plain T-shirt, curvy yoga pants. That was the real Lauren, the one with no pretention, no defenses. Those small smiles of hers. Her sideways glances when she thought he wasn't paying attention. How she ate straight out of the containers of food in his kitchen. Which would have normally bothered him with anyone else, but not her.

"What do you think, Nick?" Brandon Pulmer asked.

Nick dragged his attention away from his phone. He caught the smirk of Paulie—she knew he hadn't been listening, and she turned her iPad around so that Nick could read the last few lines of her notes. Bless her.

"It makes sense to extend the hours in the summer," Nick said. "By one hour, though, not by two. Those small-plane pilots are always pressing their luck as it is."

"Duly noted," Brandon said.

Paulie turned the iPad around and pecked at the miniature keyboard.

Nick knew that Lauren was attending a fundraising gala tonight. He'd looked it up on her website, and he wondered idly if he should attend. Some of her paintings would be up for auction, and he could add to his collection. Plus he'd be donating to a good cause of building a park in a rundown neighborhood.

He exhaled. The gala might be sold out, but there was only one way to find out. He pushed mute on the conference call, then said to Paulie, "Can you look up the Neighborhood Friends Gala and see if there's an available ticket?"

Paulie began to type away at a new screen, and Nick appreciated her efficiency. He unmuted the conference call and tried to follow along as best he could. But once Paulie gave him the thumbs up, his thoughts shifted back to Lauren as he wondered what she'd be wearing tonight. His tux should be ready to go, dry-cleaned after the last formal event he'd attended. He was sure he'd know plenty of people at the gala. Investors and donors made it a habit to attend these types of functions, not only to donate, but to see and be seen. Sort of the social night out for the who's who of San Diego.

A text came in from Tammy, and Nick exhaled. She was a woman he'd dated a few months ago, but she was too finicky for his taste.

Hey, babe, I'm coming down to San Diego this weekend. You around?

Tammy was . . . how should he explain it? A trust-fund baby who had plenty of her own money but did nothing. Unless he counted spa days and yacht outings as an occupation. In fact, he'd met her at a fundraising gala, and she'd been sweet and attentive. He'd let that go to his head, which was wrong, but sometimes it felt nice to have some undivided adulation. He'd been in a weird space since his father had recently died, and normally he wouldn't have gone out with someone as shallow as Tammy. Yet it had been nice to escape reality with her for a few hours at a time.

Now . . . he replied to her text. *I'll be around, but I'm dating someone, and I don't think she'd like me skipping out.*

There. Not exactly the full truth, but it would accomplish two things. Let Tammy down gently, and let her know that there wasn't a future between them. Besides, what were the chances of him randomly seeing her in San Diego anyway?

There was always a chance, he knew, since she was familiar with his favorite restaurants and they had some of the same acquaintances.

The conference call moved to the final agenda item, the budget.

Nick turned his phone over and pulled up the organization's financial spreadsheets. For the next hour he reviewed numbers, pushing all else out of his mind. Or at least as much as possible.

By the time he left the office, the sun was setting and he was running late. The good thing was that Paulie had told him there was a silent auction beforehand, which usually delayed things. And he was only worried about getting there for the live-auction portion that would start halfway through the dinner service.

Once he was in his tux, he drove to the event center and pulled his sports car up to the valet stand. He climbed out, noticing that he was the only one arriving. Maybe he was later than he'd thought.

"Thank you," Nick told the valet and hurried in. He hoped he hadn't missed the live auction, where Lauren's paintings would be up for bidding. At the reception table in front of the event room, he handed over a credit card and then took the bidding number they gave him.

He strolled past the reception area into the main room and saw that the lights were dimmed and a video documentary was playing about how Neighborhood Friends had helped other neighborhoods with rejuvenation projects.

Nick followed the table numbers to his assigned table while scanning the room and looking for a woman who fit Lauren's description, but he didn't see her. He sat at the only empty seat at his assigned table. The man on his right nodded a greeting, and the woman on his left gave him a broad smile. He didn't know her, but that didn't seem to stop her open friendliness.

"Hello," she said, leaning close. "I'm Gloria Roddy; who are you?"

"Nick," he said simply.

Her gaze raked over him. "Nice to meet you, Nick."

He nodded, then turned his attention to the video. After it had run its course, the lights brightened, and the MC walked to the podium. "Enjoy your dinner, ladies and gentlemen. The silent auction has now closed, and bidding for live items will start in twenty minutes."

The MC left the podium, and soft music began to play.

"So, Nick, where are you from?" Gloria said, facing him. Her spider-like, fake eyelashes fluttered.

"Mostly here," he said, then he turned to the man next to him. "You look familiar." He didn't in the least, but Nick wanted to put some sort of divide between him and Gloria.

It worked, because she started talking to the person on her other side while the meals were delivered by a host of servers. Nick kept asking John, the man to his right, more questions about his insurance agency. It worked until Nick caught sight of a woman in a red dress a couple of tables over. Tammy was here, and before he could look away, she caught his gaze.

Dread pooled in his stomach as Tammy flashed a bright smile, and he felt obligated to smile in return. Within seconds she was at his table. He rose to greet her and give her an obligatory kiss on her cheek.

"Wow, I can't believe you're here." Tammy's gaze moved to Gloria, who was watching them with open interest.

"Is this the woman you're dating?" Tammy said.

"Uh, no," Nick was quick to say. "She's . . . not here." Lauren was here, he just hadn't seen her yet. Besides, the last thing he'd do was introduce the two women.

"Aw, too bad," Tammy purred, running her hand up his arm. "Do you think she'd mind if we danced? Just once?"

Nick blinked. Sure, there was a dance floor, and a few couples who must not be hungry were dancing, but it wasn't something he was interested in doing with Tammy.

"Better not," he said. "Word might get out."

Tammy laughed. "You must be whipped, Nick. I never would have thought." Her eyes narrowed for the briefest moment. "Do you have a picture of her? I'd love to see the woman who ensnared Nicholas Matthews."

"Oh, there's Steven," Nick said, looking past her. "I should talk to him before the bidding starts." He excused himself, and as he walked away from Tammy, he felt her gaze boring into his back. So be it. But now, he had no idea where he was walking. He passed by a couple of tables, then moved toward the long tables set up for the silent auction. He didn't want to turn around to see if Tammy was still watching.

He shouldn't have come. It didn't look like Lauren was even here. Had something happened to her? He pulled out his phone and scrolled through the last text he had from her. It was from yesterday. Nothing from today, even though he'd texted her this morning.

Frustrated, he pocketed his phone, then looked up to scan the crowd a final time. His gaze paused. At the far table, a woman sat, dressed in a low-backed white dress, and although her hair was smoothed and straightened, Nick knew it was Lauren. She was talking to and smiling at the man seated next to her. Nick didn't have a good view of the man, but he could see Lauren's profile clearly. And she was beautiful.

Nick wasn't sure how long he'd been staring when the MC stood and introduced the auctioneer. Nick made his way back to his seat, which was in a location where he couldn't see Lauren anymore.

Nick retook his seat and only gave one-word answers to Gloria's questions.

He waited patiently through the bidding of the vacation packages, the pro sports memorabilia, jewelry sets, and handblown glass art.

"Next, we have a painting by local artist Lauren Ambrose," the auctioneer said. "This painting is called *Butterfly on Skyscraper*." An image of the painting displayed on the slideshow.

Nick gazed at the picture. Even if he hadn't known Lauren, the painting was something to behold. She'd put incredible, lifelike detail into the miniature of a butterfly who could have never flown so high as a fifty-story skyscraper. Or maybe it could. The juxtaposition was intriguing.

Several bidders raised their numbers, and the auctioneer listed them in turn. When the bidding slowed, around $5,000, Nick raised his auction paddle. Another woman near Lauren's table raised hers by five hundred. Nick raised his auction paddle again.

This continued for a few more interchanges, until finally Nick won out at $8,000. People in the crowd clapped as the auctioneer declared him the winning bid and went on to the next item.

Nick set his paddle down, waiting for the next Lauren Ambrose painting.

"Are you an art collector?" Gloria asked with a wide smile and a gleam in her eyes.

"Only select art," he replied, not liking the way that Gloria was appraising him.

Tammy was suddenly at his side, and when she leaned down to whisper in his ear, he nearly shot out of his chair. "Congratulations, Nick. I like a man who can appreciate the finer things of life."

"Thanks," he said, trying to keep his smile from turning into a grimace.

Tammy said something else before moving on, and Nick could only sigh with relief.

When the auctioneer announced the next Lauren Ambrose painting, Gloria tapped Nick on the arm. "You gonna bid again?"

"Yes, ma'am."

She giggled and turned her rapt attention to the front of the room. The art piece was another miniature, this one of a small puppy in the wilds of a rocky landscape. The bidding got to $7,000 before Nick raised his paddle. He won that one too, for $9,500.

His Lauren Ambrose collection was growing.

Nick waited until the next item was well underway before he rose and made his way over to the reception table. He glanced over at Lauren's table as he walked, but she was no longer in her seat. Maybe she'd left early? Or was at the restroom?

He continued to the reception area and picked up his receipts for the artwork. The woman at the desk assured him that his paintings would be specially delivered the next day to his home.

Nick strode out of the event room and headed through the lobby, when a voice stopped him.

"You following me, Mr. Matthews?"

Nick turned to see Lauren standing in the lobby, her arms folded.

15

When the bidding on her first piece of art had turned into a bidding war, Lauren had turned in her seat to see who was stirring things up. The sight of Nick sitting at one of the back tables, wearing a tux, raising a paddle to drive up the price, had made her breath stall.

And then he'd bought her second painting.

Now she faced him in the lobby, and the sight of Nicholas Matthews in a tuxedo was not for the faint of heart.

Maybe she should have just let him leave and called him later to give her a piece of her mind.

Nick slowed his pace and walked toward her. The lobby was currently empty, and the only other sound besides her thumping heart was the soft classical lobby music.

Her face heated as Nick approached, because his hazel eyes made a thorough scan of what she was wearing. She was more dressed up than she'd ever been around him, thanks to a last-minute shopping spree and being talked into this form-fitting white dress by a friendly sales lady.

Nick probably owned more than one tux and didn't have to think twice about what he'd wear to a formal gala.

"I might have known there was a small possibility you'd be here tonight," he said in that deep voice of his, his lips twitching.

Lauren wasn't going to give in and smile. She kept her arms folded. "You spent almost twenty grand on my paintings. Do you like throwing money around?"

Nick didn't seem perturbed at her question; in fact, he stepped closer and lowered his voice. "Money toward a good cause. Did you see the plans for the neighborhood park? Really tugged at my heart strings."

Lauren brought her hand to her mouth, but she was too late to stop her laugh. "I can see that you're still teary-eyed."

Nick did smile then, and Lauren told her heart to be still.

"You can't blame me for bidding, especially when you're the one who's donating your time and talents. Neither of which I have much of, so I have to come up with the next best thing. Cash."

Lauren smirked. "Is that why so many women were flocking around you?"

At this, Nick looked surprised, then he slowly raised his brow. "You were spying on me?"

Lauren forbade herself to blush. "It was hard not to look over at the guy who kept outbidding everyone." She stared into his hazel eyes. "Tell me, how many girlfriends do you have here tonight?"

"I don't have a girlfriend," he said, his gaze dropping to her mouth.

Right. "Just friends with benefits?"

He released a slow breath. "One woman I talked to is someone I dated for a little bit, but I told her I wasn't available anymore."

"Oh? Why not?" Lauren knew she was outright flirting with Nick, but she couldn't seem to stop herself.

"I've been preoccupied as of late." His gaze dropped to her mouth again, and that did all kinds of crazy things to her pulse.

"With what?" Had her voice dropped to a whisper?

"Buying art." He winked.

Lauren swallowed and unfolded her arms. "Well, now you have yourself quite the collection."

He leaned close, close enough that she felt the warmth of his breath against her ear when he said, "Do you want to dance, Lauren Ambrose?"

She didn't move. "You're kidding."

He drew back, his eyes appraising. "Do I look like I'm kidding?"

No. Not at all. "I'm not interested in dancing."

"Why not?" he said, not moving back or giving her any space to think clearly. His scent, his presence, his voice, his intense gaze, all created a slow buzz that traveled through her body.

"Because . . ."

A single eyebrow arched as he waited for her to continue. Apparently she'd been rendered mute. His hand brushed hers, then his fingers curled around her fingers. "One dance. I think we owe it to ourselves to find out."

"Find out what?" she rasped, her voice unsteady.

"Why I keep buying your paintings."

Her thoughts raced, her body felt numb, her feet and legs weightless. If she danced with Nick, she might find out for herself how real this thing was budding between them. Or maybe it wasn't real at all.

He hadn't released her hand, and he kept a hold of it after she nodded. They walked back into the event room, where the auction had ended and several couples had taken to the dance floor. Others were socializing. Some preparing to leave.

As they reached the dance floor, Lauren suddenly had the sense that Nick would be a good dancer. And she was right.

She rested one hand lightly on his shoulder. The other hand was enfolded in his warm one. She was hyperaware of his hand resting at the top of her hip. He wasn't holding her all that close yet, but his slow, casual movements as they danced had her pulse thumping.

He was a natural, and she was not. It was hardly fair that this beautiful, successful man, who seemed to be working his way into her every sense, was also good at dancing.

"You *are* dancing," a woman's voice cut into Lauren's hazy thoughts.

Nick turned his head. "I guess I changed my mind. Either that, or I couldn't say no."

The woman was the same one Lauren had seen talking to Nick earlier. Her red dress was tight and emphasized her generous bosom. Her platinum-blond hair and glittering diamonds made no secret of her wealth.

The woman laughed, then gazed at Lauren. "Is this her?" she asked Nick.

"It is," Nick said, squeezing Lauren's hand as if he were trying to send her a message.

"Hi, I'm Lauren," she said.

"Tammy," the woman in red said. Then she frowned. "Lauren Ambrose, the artist?"

It wasn't often that people recognized her name, but her paintings had been auctioned off here.

Tammy's gaze cut to Nick. "What does your mother think?" She laughed, and it was a conspiratorial laugh. "Remember when you blew me off? Because your mother was hung up on you getting together with Chelsey? Someone she could use as her puppet. How did you get away with dating someone else?"

Nick's answering smile seemed forced. "Mind if we get back to our dance?"

"Oh sure, sure," Tammy said, patting Nick on the arm. "I wouldn't want to *intrude*."

When she left, Lauren was confused.

"Who's Chelsey?" she asked.

"A family friend whom my mother thinks she has the right to match me with," he said. "Both Chelsey and I agree that we'd never be a good match."

Lauren had no choice but to believe him. "But you dated Tammy?"

Nick grimaced. "Don't remind me."

"I mean . . . she's pretty, but—"

Nick moved his hand from her hip to her back, so that now she was pressed against him. She forgot what she was going to say. He lowered his head and spoke against her ear. "Let's forget about Tammy and everything she said. I like this song."

Lauren hadn't been paying attention to the specific songs, but the current one was nice. She closed her eyes as Nick released her hand and slipped it behind her back as well. So now both of her arms were looped about his neck as they moved together in a slow circle.

It took her a moment to realize he was humming to the music. She wanted to laugh, but she was also kind of enjoying his humming too. She sighed into him, reveling in this moment, which couldn't go on forever. Reality was waiting for her, and she knew as well as she knew anything, Nick was a very tempting man . . . but there was no future for them.

When the song changed, Lauren drew away slightly. Nick met her gaze with a half-smile, one that told her she was on his mind. And that he was enjoying the dancing too.

"What did she mean about your mom?" Lauren asked.

"Ignore everything that Tammy said," he answered.

Lauren tilted her head. "You're seriously not going to tell me?"

His gaze traveled over her face. "My mom gets a little wound up when I date someone. Puts them through the full-court press. She's scared off more than one person in my life."

"What did Tammy mean about your mom wanting a puppet?"

Nick exhaled. "My mom's co-owner of a trust my dad set up for me should something happen to me. When I marry, it will transfer to my wife, and my mother will be left with her annual salary. Which is no small thing, but right now, she has a lot more access to funds."

Lauren swallowed. "Oh, wow."

"Yeah, she can be a little intense," he said. "I'm a little scared of her myself."

Lauren smiled. "Well, good thing I don't have to worry about meeting her."

Nick moved his hands up her back. "Why would you say that?"

"Because we're not dating."

Nick's hands continued their slow journey up her back. "We could change that."

Lauren heard what he'd said, but it took a moment for the words to register. "Don't say things like that."

He drew back to meet her gaze. "Why not?"

She grimaced. "You know why. You of all people know the truth."

They'd stopped dancing, although the music still swirled about them. "What if there was no curse, Lauren?" he asked in a quiet voice.

His eyes were darker in the lighting on the dance floor. He must have shaved just before coming tonight, because his jaw looked smooth. And that quirk of his lips was becoming all too familiar.

She moved her hands to the tops of his shoulders. "I guess we'll never find out, will we?" Her hands continued down until they rested against his chest. "Thanks for the dance, but I need to get going. Big day tomorrow."

"Oh? Lots of stuff?"

She couldn't help her smile. "Exactly."

He seemed to want to say something else, but then changed his mind. He released his hold on her. "Can I walk you to your car?"

She liked it better when his arms had been around her, but this was smarter. Much wiser. And she should really turn him down, because more time spent with Nicholas Matthews was becoming something she was starting to crave. It was better to keep her distance. "To the valet?"

He shrugged. "Wherever you want me to *take you.*"

She didn't miss the flash of concern in his eyes. He'd been amazing about helping her through the Kevin fiasco. And truthfully, she was still nervous alone in her condo, for the simple fact that Kevin knew where she lived. Not that she'd admit it to Nick or anyone else. The protective order was in place, and she'd have to trust in that.

She stepped away from him, and this time he didn't try to take her hand. They wove through the milling people, and Nick was stopped several times, but he quickly waved people off. By the time they reached the lobby, Lauren was wondering if there was anyone Nick *didn't* know. Plenty of the gazes had been on her, and she didn't miss the interest and speculation.

Lauren walked outside, with Nick close behind. While she waited for the valet to bring her car, Nick asked, "No contact from Kevin?"

"No," Lauren said. "Nothing since the last time you asked me this morning."

She sensed his smile even though she wasn't looking at him. The valet had just turned into the circular driveway with her car.

"It's not like you're very forthcoming with information," he said in a low voice. "I think your record is a three-word text."

That made her look over at him. "Are you analyzing me?"

He gave a small nod. "I've been analyzing you since before I even met you."

For some reason a rash of goose bumps rose on her arms.

"And what are your findings?" she asked.

The valet climbed out of her car, but her gaze was still focused on Nick.

"Inconclusive as of now," he said. "If you don't like texting as a form of communication, what do you like?"

"Well, I don't usually answer the phone."

"So, in person then?"

She gave a small shrug. "It depends." She took the keys from the valet and handed over a couple of bills.

He thanked her, and she turned to look at Nick again. "Thanks for coming and bidding on my art."

He'd slipped his hands in his pockets. "Any time."

The comment was off the cuff, but she sensed he meant it. Well, she couldn't stand here all night, with the valet as their audience. So she told Nick good night and climbed into her car. As she drove away, she caught a glimpse of him, still standing in the same place, watching after her.

16

"Have you even listened to a word I've said?" Nick's mom asked.

That caught his attention. "Of course," he murmured.

"Then what time will you be there?"

Where? he wanted to ask, but he was pretty sure she'd be offended. Besides, she'd mentioned an email, so he'd pull it up and figure out which event his mother was talking about. She was forever throwing fundraising events, and when he told her about going to the Neighborhood Friends one last week, she'd been thrilled.

He did a search on his mom's name in his email. *Restore the Old Mission Home in San Clemente* read the title. Too close to fly and too inconvenient to drive.

Besides, the event was Sunday night, and he had early morning conference calls on Monday, as in two in the morning.

"I don't think—" he began.

"Don't you dare back out on me, young man," his mother cut in. "You said you'd support me, and I'm expecting it. Oh, and Chelsey will be there."

"Mom—"

"I know what you're about to say," she cut in. "But Chelsey just came off a terrible breakup, and I was talking to her mother, and we think she's matured. You should see her now, Nick. She got those hair extensions, and they really compliment her."

"Mom," he cut in with a firm voice. "I'm dating someone, and I planned to bring her."

His mom went silent for a full thirty seconds.

Nick's heart thumped at the white lie . . . if he couldn't convince Lauren to come, then he'd back out of the event and deal with his mother's wrath later.

"Does the woman you're bringing happen to be Lauren Ambrose?"

Nick froze. "What did you say?"

"Oh, don't be coy with me, son," his mother said. "Tammy and I had a long chat this morning. She told me all about the artist you're dating. And I did some searching on the internet, and I must say—"

"You looked up Lauren?" he asked, not sure if he was impressed or completely annoyed. And what had Tammy been doing calling his mom?

"I did, and you can do better, son," his mother said.

Nick was too stunned to speak.

"Chelsey is cultured, she has an MFA, and she's well-connected," his mom continued. "I'm not even sure if Lauren Ambrose went to college. Whatever she did, she's in a dead-end profession. Her paintings are so tiny. No one can see them. So I'm sorry to say that I don't approve."

Nick found his voice. "I didn't *ask* for your approval."

His mother's next words were lighter. "How serious is it?" He could hear the hope in her voice, the hope that he'd tell her it wasn't serious at all.

But if there was one thing Nick couldn't do, it was hide his emotions from his mother. She had the uncanny ability to discern what he was feeling even through a phone conversation. "Well, I like her, but she doesn't want much to do with me."

His mother chuckled. "Goodness, that's *interesting*. I guess your good looks, charming personality, and millions of dollars aren't good enough for her? Like I said, she's not for you, Nicholas."

Nick wanted to call Tammy right now and tell her to stay out of his life for good. "I hope that anyone I date will look past my money."

His mother scoffed. "You can hope, but it won't happen. People are shallow. And they don't change."

Nick found himself holding his breath, hoping his mother wouldn't go into a tirade about his father. Thankfully, she hadn't since his death. It appeared she greatly respected the deceased. It was one of his mother's biggest complaints—that all the associates surrounding his father were shallow and obtuse. And she could truly go on for hours about all of her opinions on the matter.

"Lauren isn't shallow," Nick said, hardly believing that he was discussing this with his mother in the first place. "In fact, she has her own money, but her life is very complicated." That was the best he could come up with.

"She's an artist, which means she probably spends her day dabbing brushes into paint. *So* productive. Besides, you said she doesn't care for you," his mother said in a frank tone. "What do you see in *her* then?"

Nick smiled to himself, still amazed he was in this conversation in the first place. "She's not at all like Tammy, that's for sure. And I've told you more than once that Chelsey and I aren't going to ever get together. Lauren is unassuming. She's the master of her own fate. She's stubborn. Beautiful. And she puts everyone and everything before herself."

His mother went quiet again.

Nick began to wonder if their connection had been broken when she said, "Bring her to San Clemente. I've changed my mind. I want to meet her after all. Just know that Chelsey will be there, and I hope that you will treat her well."

After hanging up with his mother, Nick lowered his head and rubbed at his temples. No. This couldn't happen. He and Lauren weren't really dating . . . he hadn't even kissed her. So there was no way he'd ask her to meet his mother—Lauren would be scared off—assuming there was something between the two of them to be scared off about.

Nick mulled this over. They weren't in a relationship, so how could she be scared off?

Maybe he should text her to see if she was available Sunday. He'd find some way to make it more about going to see art along the way? He typed a few things into his laptop, googling art museums between San Diego and San Clemente.

Well, there it was. Another reason to invite her.

But instead of texting her or calling, Nick decided to do something that was unprecedented for him. He didn't even know if she was home, and he'd have to use the gate code she'd given him that night she'd been worried about Kevin lurking. But Nick was determined to show up on her doorstep and ask her in person. Flowers might help too.

Which was why, thirty minutes later, he found himself at a neighborhood florist shop, staring at too many choices. What type of flowers did a woman like Lauren like? Exotic? Bold? Or sweet? Were roses too pretentious and daisies too childish? He settled on some white lilies, because their elegant grace reminded him of Lauren.

The afternoon sun was warmer than usual when Nick stood at Lauren's door. He rang the doorbell and waited a couple of minutes. No one came, so he rang it one more time. Still nothing. He debated whether to leave the flowers on the doorstep. He didn't have a note on them, but he could text her later. So he set them in front of the door, and just as he turned away, the door cracked open.

"Nick?"

He turned.

Lauren was wearing a pale-pink tank shirt and some ratty shorts. Her hair was pulled into a messy ponytail, swept off her graceful neck. She had a sleepy look about her, which was pretty darn sexy.

"Were you asleep?" he asked. "Sorry to wake you."

"I wasn't asleep," she said. "I was painting."

Now he noticed the bits of paint on her tank shirt and the one hand that he could see.

"No suit or tie?" She openly appraised him, which only made him feel extra warm. "Khakis are a nice change."

"I can be casual sometimes."

She didn't look convinced, but her gaze was amused, then she looked down to her feet, where the flowers were. "You brought flowers?" She looked up at him. "Why?"

He slid his hands into his pockets. "Does a man need a reason to bring a beautiful woman flowers?"

Her eyes narrowed, and she set a hand on that curvy hip of hers. "You're going with that, Nick?"

His smile slipped out. "I wanted to, uh, ask you out, and I thought that flowers would work in my favor."

Lauren's lips parted as if she was going to speak, but then she hesitated.

Nick stepped closer and picked up the vase. Then he handed it to her. "You can keep them even if you turn me down. They reminded me of you anyway, so it wouldn't really work to keep them at my house. Because I'd just be reminded of how you turned me down."

She bit her bottom lip, but her eyes were amused. "Want to come in? See what masterpiece I'm working on that you'll probably buy for ten grand?"

He chuckled. "Lead the way."

She stepped back and opened the door wider.

He passed by her, catching her scent of wildflowers, and paint, mixed with lilies. She shut the door, then she took the flowers to the coffee table, where she moved over a few magazines. She set the vase in the middle of the table, then straightened.

Nick watched her movements, thinking maybe he should have texted her after all. Lauren had an intoxicating effect on him, and being alone with her, battling his thoughts, was entering the danger zone. Soft music played from one of the back rooms, something classical.

Lauren turned to face him, a small smile on her face, which only made her look more lovely. "Why did you say the lilies remind you of me?"

He glanced at the flowers, then back to her face. Maybe he should be honest and see where it took him. She'd invited him in, so that said something, right?

"The petals are smooth like your skin," he said. Lauren's eyes widened. "And their color innocent white like your heart." He paused, and Lauren's mouth twitched as if she was holding back a smile or laugh. He was so enjoying this. "And . . . their fragrance is subtle like your personality."

The line between her brows appeared. "Did you google that?"

"What?" Nick sputtered. "No. I might be a trained accountant, but I can string together a few words."

She smiled, and his heart melted. When she moved toward him, he could only stare. And when she grasped his arms and rose up on her toes to kiss his cheek, he couldn't remember why he'd been second-guessing coming over here.

What would she do if he pulled her into his arms and kissed her like he'd imagined for far too long?

But Lauren had already moved away, leaving a whisper of her presence behind.

He followed her down the hallway to a bedroom that had been converted into a studio. The music grew louder, and Nick asked, "You like classical?"

"Some of it," Lauren said. "I'm not too picky, but I'm sort of old-fashioned when it comes to music."

Nick stepped into the studio after Lauren. The room had no carpet, and several easels were scattered throughout the room. The room glowed nearly orange with the setting sun coming through the tall windows. The room smelled of paint, wildflowers, and Lauren. Blotches of paint speckled the floor, and everything had a warm, cozy feeling, like he'd stepped back in time to an old painter's studio.

Lauren moved among the half-finished paintings, pointing out some of the details. Nick was listening to all of her explanations, but he was mostly watching her. The tilt of her head, the quirk of her lips, and how she wrinkled her nose when he complimented her. How she moved away each time he closed the distance.

"I paint in layers," she said. "Then I let each layer dry on its own. So one miniature can take two weeks to complete because of the drying time."

He nodded. "Which is why you have so many in process at the same time?"

Her blue eyes connected with his. "Right."

His hands went back into his pockets, and he kept them there. The music playlist she had running switched to a mellow jazz number. "Do you take requests?"

"Um, I don't know." Her mouth quirked.

"You don't *know*?" he said, moving closer again. "Either you do or you don't."

"I haven't been asked before." She shrugged and moved away again.

Before she could bypass him, he grasped her hand. "Well, think about it," he said in a low voice. "Because I'd like to make a request."

She looked up at him; she was so close that he could see the beating pulse at the hollow of her neck.

"Tell me what it is, and then I'll let you know."

"I haven't decided yet," he said. "I just know I want to make one."

She laughed, and he grinned. And she wasn't moving away from him or releasing his hand, which made him doubly glad.

"Okay, when you decide, let me know." Her eyes clung to his, and he wondered if her heart was beating as hard as his was.

"Okay," he said.

"Okay." She smirked. "Why didn't you text me, Mr. Matthews? I know you're a busy man."

"I'm a very busy man," he agreed, still holding her gaze. "But you said you don't like texting."

"That's because I have other things to do."

"I'm well aware of that, and so I was wondering if you had time to go for a drive on Sunday."

She pursed her lips. "A drive? That sounds really vague."

"There's a little more to it than that, sweetheart." He slipped his fingers through hers, testing, waiting.

She inched closer. "Will food be involved?"

"Yes."

"Okay."

He was surprised and elated, which might have explained his next impulsive move. He released her hand and cradled her face, barely touching her. She wasn't drawing away, and her soft smile was the best invitation he could imagine. So he kissed her.

Gently at first, because the last thing he wanted to do was startle her with the emotions clashing inside of him. Her lips were soft, warm, just as he knew they'd be, and she tasted sweet. He drew away a few inches to find that her eyes were closed.

So he kissed her again, and this time she slid her arms around his waist.

The feel of her body pressed against his was something his accountant mind couldn't adequately describe as she relaxed into him and kissed him back, exploring and tasting him equally as he was her. He moved his hands behind her neck and buried his fingers in her long hair. The softness only heightened his senses, and he knew he couldn't keep this kiss innocent for much longer. Reluctantly, he gave her a final, lingering kiss. Then he rested his forehead against hers.

She slid her hands around his torso and up his chest, then drew away. Still, her eyes were closed, and their rapid breathing seemed to match.

"Nick," she whispered. "We can't be doing this."

"But we are," he countered.

"Then we should stop. Now." But her tone had no conviction behind it.

"Okay, you stop first."

She laughed and slid her arms around his neck, pulling him closer. He obliged, and his mouth found hers again.

Nick didn't know how much time they spent kissing in the middle of her studio, but by the time they both decided they *really* had to stop, the sun had set and the purples of twilight swathed the room.

"I need to tell you something." Nick slid his hands down her arms, then linked both of her hands with his.

Her blue eyes were hazy, and her lips were swollen with his thorough kissing. He didn't think she could be more beautiful than she was at this moment.

"I hope it's something good."

"Well, that depends on how you look at it," Nick said. "Our drive on Sunday has a destination."

A line appeared between Lauren's brows. "Not food?"

"There will be food, but it's a fundraiser gala for literacy awareness in conjunction with my mother's magazine, and she's the hostess."

17

Lauren stared at Nick as he told her that his mother was going to be part of their outing on Sunday.

"I thought I'd bring you," he said, "and she could meet you, and—"

"Wait." Lauren placed two fingers on his mouth because all of this was hard to comprehend. "You want me to meet your *mother*? We haven't even been on a date."

Nick got that sheepish look on his face, the one that was kind of adorable. Not to mention the tilt of his lips—lips she was now very familiar with and wouldn't mind kissing again. But to meet his mother?

Tammy's words returned, about some woman—Chelsey—whom his mother apparently wanted him to get together with and probably even marry.

"I don't think so," Lauren said. "I mean, I think we should date more before that happens. Or really . . . we shouldn't be dating at all. You know how complicated things are—"

He didn't seem to be listening, because he only pulled her into his arms again and then started kissing her neck.

"I can't think straight when you do that," she said, already breathless.

"That's the point," he murmured.

His breath tickled, and she squirmed with laughter, but his hold was solid, and all she accomplished was edging closer to his warm, solid torso. Which was pretty much heaven.

She supposed that spending so much time with this man—handsome, charming, interested in everything she told him, not to mention his protectiveness over her—would lead to a kiss or two . . . But she was pretty much feeling like he'd found a way into her heart. And that was the last thing she could let happen. No matter that he knew her past, her family's curse, and all the complications that brought; he didn't seem to mind.

His phone buzzed, and although he ignored it, Lauren said, "I think that's a sign. You know, you should stop kissing me, and I should get back to work."

He lifted his head and with one hand took his phone out of his pocket and turned off the ringer. "I think you have too many rules."

"I'm practical."

Nick smiled. "Which could be considered a blessing or a curse."

"Whatever," she said with a laugh.

He linked their hands, although his closeness made her want to continue the kissing that he'd started.

"So . . . can I pick you up Sunday?" he asked.

She bit her lip. Sunday suddenly felt far away, but it would be completely impractical to suggest that she'd like to see him before Sunday. "I'm thinking about it."

His gaze moved over her face, and the longing in his eyes made heat pool deep in her belly. "I could kiss you again," he said in a low voice.

She'd been thoroughly kissed by this man already, yet he was still making her blush. "I don't take bribes."

Nick chuckled and pulled her against him, wrapping his arms about her shoulders. "I think I'm learning that you'll never be easy to convince of anything. So I guess I'll exercise my infinite patience and hope for the best."

He smelled so wonderful that she almost gave in right then and there. But she truly wanted to think about his suggestion while not in his intoxicating presence.

Her heart wasn't in any hurry for him to leave, but her mind was telling her something else. More accurately, warning her.

By the time Nick left her condo, Lauren felt like her world had shifted. For better or for worse, she didn't know yet. After locking the double bolts on her door, she sank onto the living room couch and tucked her feet beneath her. Wrapping her arms about herself, she closed her eyes. She imagined Nick climbing into that expensive sports car of his, driving back to his multimillion-dollar beach house. Running companies all across the world. Making deals left and right. Traveling to Italy.

Living. Really living.

Her life was centered in a small condo, littered with paints and canvases, as she created works of juxtaposition. Yes, she could live a bigger life if she wanted to. Her bank account could definitely support a lifestyle to rival any millionaire, but the thought of putting herself out there, beyond the occasional gallery event or fundraising dinner, was daunting.

She wasn't charismatic. She was private. She liked the quiet. And she liked being able to take each day as it came and not chase the almighty agenda.

Nick was so . . . opposite of her. Yet the touch of his hands at her waist, the warmth of his mouth, the urgency of his kisses, the way that his hazel eyes captured hers . . . Her skin buzzed, even now, as she thought about him.

Nick was a temptation, an intoxicating ambrosia. That was all.

So. Maybe she should go with him Sunday. Meet his mother. Prove to herself that their worlds could never coexist. Based on what little Tammy had implied, Nick's mother wouldn't care for Lauren. And any woman in her right mind wouldn't come between a man and his closest family member.

Besides, Lauren couldn't allow herself to believe that Nick saw her as anything more than a short-term conquest. A fling, maybe. She'd intrigued him because she wasn't the norm, and maybe he'd been taken off center by that. So he was curious. Just like she was curious about him.

She hadn't really expected his humor, his generosity, or his attention to detail—his attention to *her.*

Her gaze landed on the vase of lilies on her coffee table. They were so elegant, so purely white, it was hard to believe they were a real, living plant. Almost untouchable. She was far from what he described, and although she knew her own flaws inside and out, it was as if he looked past all of them.

"Nick," she breathed. "What am I going to do about you? Things between us are impossible."

When her phone buzzed, she startled in the quiet. She pulled the phone from her pocket, and her heart fluttered without her permission when she saw the text from Nick.

Still thinking? he'd written.

She read it a couple of times, unable to stop the smile on her face. He must have just returned to his beach house, and she was still on his mind.

She wrote back: *Are you putting me on a deadline, Mr. Matthews?*

It was flirty, and it wasn't helping her reluctance. But her heart didn't seem to care about her mind's warnings.

No deadline, but I'll be checking in every hour.

Lauren laughed. Then she typed: *Don't you have something better to do?*

I have a lot of things to do, but I have my priorities as well.

She was blushing again. And she was now wishing she hadn't chased him out of her condo so soon. With a sigh, she rose to her feet. It was nearly dark, and she'd already put in a full day of painting, so maybe she'd call it a night. Order takeout, stream a movie, and think about what it would be like not to have a curse hanging over her head.

Instead, she spent the next hour scrolling through websites, looking at dresses. Something that she might wear *if* she were to go with Nick on Sunday. Was his mother a traditional, formal person? Or was she flamboyant, with streaks of color in her hair and gobs of jewelry?

Lauren paused when she saw a strappy peach dress. It wasn't too formal, and it was pretty in a summery way. She loved it. Without analyzing her thought process, she clicked on the order button and selected one-day delivery. It wasn't her normal style to be so impulsive, but suddenly she wanted to see Nick's face when he saw her in that dress.

Assuming she would go.

She closed the browser and opened her Kindle app to pull up a historical novel she'd started the week before. As of now, she was ninety-nine percent sure she'd go with Nick to his mother's event. But . . . she'd make him wait until tomorrow to find out.

Lauren woke up early, even before the birds. She turned over in the dark and faced the window of her bedroom. The grayness of the light coming in told her that dawn was approaching. She thought about the day before, when Nick had come over and brought her flowers. And had then kissed her.

She waited for the regret to form. For her nerves to get the better of her. But she only felt warm and content. She wanted to see Nick again, and she wondered if he was awake right now. Or maybe he was sleeping because of another middle-of-the-night conference call.

She lifted her phone from the nightstand next to her bed and scrolled through the texts from the night before. They made her smile again. She thought of the dress she'd ordered and express shipped.

Realizing that she wanted to go with Nick, even if it meant meeting his mother, Lauren closed her eyes, allowing herself to feel what she was feeling. She liked Nick, a lot. Would going with him only set herself up for future disappointment?

Maybe she could consider this date as casual and fun. With no commitments or expectation. If things went further, then she'd have to put a stop to that in order to protect her heart. Because Nick definitely had the potential to be a heartbreaker.

Lauren looked at the text strand again, then typed in a message: *I bought a dress.*

She didn't expect him to be awake, let alone reply right away. But the three dots of his reply danced on her screen before a message popped up.

Good morning to you too.

Lauren smiled, her skin heating. *You're up early,* she wrote.

I'm up late, he replied. *I haven't gone to sleep yet.*

Sorry, am I keeping you awake?

Her phone rang. Well, she couldn't ignore it or pretend she was busy when they were in the middle of a text conversation. Her pulse thrummed regardless.

"Hi," she said. She hoped he couldn't hear the breathlessness in that single word.

"What color's the dress?" Nick's deep voice rasped over the phone. Not because he'd just woken up, but because he hadn't gone to bed yet.

"Peach."

She heard the smile in his voice when he said, "Does three o'clock work?"

"Why so early?" She relaxed on her pillows and gazed up at the ceiling.

"I want to make a couple of stops along the way."

She exhaled, trying to keep her heart rate mellow. "Like what?"

"Can a man not have any surprises?"

Lauren smiled. "Okay, three works."

18

Nick sat in his car for a few moments after pulling into Lauren's condo parking lot, trying to analyze how he felt. Nervous. It was an unnatural feeling for him. He couldn't remember the last time he'd been nervous about something. But he guessed that the prospect of introducing a woman, specifically Lauren Ambrose, to his mother had done it.

The fundraising gala was dressy but not formal, so instead of a suit coat, he simply wore a shirt and tie. But it wasn't his own choice of clothing he was thinking about, it was what Lauren might be wearing. He hadn't seen her since the day he'd dropped in on her. The day they'd kissed.

Nick already had eclectic sleeping hours, but after kissing Lauren, he'd taken insomnia to a whole new level. Even doubling the miles he usually ran hadn't helped. There was nothing for it but to see her again. He just hoped that she'd be mellow about what he had to tell her on the drive.

About an hour ago, he'd answered a call from her grandmother, and well, things were about to change.

Nick climbed out of the car and headed to Lauren's front door. He was on time, and he was sure that Lauren would be ready. She didn't do much by halves. But when he rang the doorbell, there was no answer. He waited a few moments, then knocked.

The door opened a crack, and he caught a glimpse of her blue eyes and the fact that she was wearing a towel. "Hi," Lauren said. "I'm sort of running late. Do you mind waiting outside?"

"Uh, no . . ."

The door shut.

Nick blinked. Okay, then. He paced away from the front door and gazed out over the condo property. There wasn't a soul in sight, and he guessed everyone was enjoying a lazy Sunday. The minutes ticked by, and Nick turned to the most recent emails on his phone. He replied to a couple of them.

Then the door cracked open again. "Do you think you can help me?" Lauren asked.

Nick looked over at her. "Sure." She was dressed now, and well, she looked beautiful. She'd swept her hair from her neck and arranged it into a chignon. Silver earrings dangled from her ears, matching the silver chain she always wore.

Her dress was definitely peach, and the thin straps exposed her smooth shoulders. The bodice dipped low enough that for the first time he saw the heart-shaped pendant at the end of her necklace. The skirt of the dress flared over her hips, following her curves as if the dress had been custom-made for her body. The length hit her mid-thigh, giving Nick a good dose of her long legs and the fact that she was still barefoot. *Eyes up,* he commanded himself.

"You look beautiful," he said, although it felt like an understatement.

Lauren gave him a half smile. "You look nice yourself. No jacket?"

"No jacket."

He didn't know what she needed help with, but he should keep his hands to himself. She opened the door wider, and he stepped in. She smelled like fresh flowers, and he wondered if it was too soon to kiss her right now or if he should wait until the end of their date.

Lauren pushed the door closed, then turned her back to him. The zipper on the dress was halfway up. Which gave him a view of her back. He swallowed.

"Can you finish zipping me up?" Lauren asked, looking over her shoulder at him. "This dress runs small, and I can't get it to zip. I might have to change."

Nick could help her out. Yes. He stepped forward, and grasped the zipper tab. But that also put him closer to Lauren and her tempting skin. He moved up the zipper, and although it was snug, the dress zipped closed. But he didn't step away, because what would one small kiss hurt?

He rested his hands on her bare shoulders, then pressed his mouth on her neck.

"Did I tell you that you look beautiful?" he whispered.

"You did," she said.

He kissed her shoulder. She exhaled and leaned against him. Then he ran his hands over her arms and settled at her waist.

Lauren slipped her hands over his, and they linked fingers. She felt heavenly in his arms, and he breathed her in.

"Are you trying to butter me up before meeting your mom?" she asked.

Nick chuckled. "No, my intentions are pure." He hadn't meant to sound so serious, but that's how it came out.

Lauren noticed, and she turned in his arms. He kept his hands at her waist because he wasn't ready to let her go yet.

"What *are* your intentions, Nicholas Matthews?" she asked, her lake-blue eyes connecting with his.

Her tone was light, but he sensed her question to be sincere. And leading. "My intentions are to get to know you better. And since I can't stop thinking about you, I want to figure out if we should be . . . seeing each other more."

She rested her hands on his forearms, bringing them a tad closer. "You know I only date casually."

"I know." His gaze dipped to her mouth. "What are the chances of me changing your mind?"

Her eyes sparkled. "I guess we'll find out."

He lifted her necklace and gazed at the heart pendant. "You always wear this."

"My grandmother gave it to me when I was sixteen," Lauren said. "She believes it's good luck. And if I take it off, the family curse has more power."

He ran his thumb over the face of the pendant. "Do you ever take it off?"

"No."

Nick gazed at her. "Never?"

She shook her head, then wrapped her fingers over his hand that was holding the pendant. "Not even in the shower."

He tried not to let his mind go there, but the brush of her body against his was making it a difficult feat. "I want to hear the legend."

Her brows lifted. "Why?"

"So I can figure out how to break the curse," he said.

"It won't matter," she said. "I once tried to talk to my grandma into burning candles at the church to reciting spells. She just scoffed at that."

"Sounds like we have more research to do."

Her mouth tilted upward. "You really think you could break the curse once and for all?"

"I guess we'll find out," he said, lowering his head and tasting her mouth.

"Nick," she murmured against his mouth even as she kissed him back. "You can't be serious."

"I'm very serious." Kissing Lauren told him one thing. She wanted him too. And that was enough for him, for now, but he had every intention of digging deep into the Ambrose Estate. Both literally and figuratively. As much as he'd like to stay in her condo forever and keep kissing her, they needed to get on the road, and he needed to tell her about the progression of the contract with her grandmother.

But Lauren's arms twined about his neck, and her body pressed against his as she slowly kissed him back, so Nick decided to stay in this bubble a little while longer. But there was one question that was plaguing him. How did her sister Sofia and her boyfriend manage to avoid the "curse"?

"We need to get going," Nick whispered against Lauren's neck.

"Mmm."

"Lauren."

She opened her eyes, and her gaze told him that they were about to cross the line into feeling emotions that, according to Lauren, she refused to entertain.

He released his hold on her and stepped away. Her cheeks were flushed, and she blinked a couple of times. "Okay, let me grab my things."

He smiled at the breathlessness of her voice. And as he watched her cross to the kitchen table to retrieve her multicolored bag and her cell phone, he shoved his hands in his pockets so that he wouldn't pull her into another kiss.

Once they were in his sports car and on the freeway, heading north, he put the car onto cruise control, then reached for her hand. Their fingers linked naturally, comfortably. And Nick wasn't sure if his heart rate would ever go down around Lauren.

But he couldn't wait any longer to tell her about Ambrose. "When's the last time you talked to your grandmother or Sofia?" He immediately felt the tension in her hand. He glanced over at her and found her blues eyes on him.

"I haven't talked to my grandmother," Lauren said. "Sofia and I have texted a little. A phone call from Lillian Ambrose is usually an emergency. And Sofia and I have never been . . . close."

He nodded. "I understand. And I should probably let Sofia tell you about this, but since we're, uh, dating . . ."

The edges of her mouth lifted, but her eyes looked worried.

"Your grandmother and I are in contract negotiations," he said, putting it all out there as quickly and concisely as possible. "She turned down the initial offer, but I followed up a couple of days later with some revisions. She and Sofia sent over an entire list of demands. Some were potential deal breakers, but we have found common ground and have both made some compromises."

He stole another glance at Lauren. She was still holding his hand, so that was a good sign, but her eyes had narrowed. "What exactly are you asking my grandmother for, Nick?"

He exhaled. Okay. Here it was. "Thirty percent, but I'm the primary investor. I have three others on board, and we are sinking in all the up-front financing. Predictions are that it will take four or five months to have the operation running and six months before we see income. Another three months before there's profit. I won't pull dividends until the twelve-month mark, which gives a ninety day cushion for reevaluation on all fronts. Sofia insisted on that, and I agreed."

Lauren stared straight ahead, not saying a thing.

"You understand the political climate in our country and the oil and gas crisis," Nick said in a quieter voice. "This new technology will be a forerunner, and I'm currently working to add the Ambrose company on the patent. That will be the final piece in the process. Your grandmother said that if the company is named as a partner on the patent, then she will sign."

Lauren's voice was small when she said, "What does that mean for Ambrose?"

"It means . . . that if this technology eases the crises by superior oil excavation, then by owning the only patented machinery and software, your grandmother could become the wealthiest woman in the nation."

Lauren exhaled, then closed her eyes.

Nick had given her the basics; although there were still a thousand tiny details, she now knew the gist of it all.

"Money always talks, doesn't it?" Lauren said, her eyes still closed.

Nick rubbed his thumb over her hand. "Money motivates. It's a mover and shaker. Money can be used for good. Money can save a nation. Restore it to independence. The technology that I've invested in is not an anomaly. Someone else will come up with something similar. There's no reason your grandmother shouldn't be the forerunner instead of someone else. She's worked her entire life in this industry, sometimes white-knuckling it in a business world not accepting of female CEOs. This could be your grandmother, or I could take it to another landowner."

Lauren nodded and opened her eyes.

"It's not a threat, Lauren; it's a fact," he said in a soft voice. "And it's only business."

"Business that could change the face of America's economy."

"That too."

Her smile was sad. "My grandmother built an empire on her own. She played the rules until she could make her own. Bringing in you, with so much investment power, feels like a step backward."

Nick could understand how Lauren would say that, although he saw it differently. He brought her hand to his lips and pressed a kiss there. "I'm going to take good care of your grandmother, Lauren."

Her gaze met his, and he hated that her eyes were watering.

"But I also want you to know that if you think I should back off, I will." He swallowed at the words that had come out of his mouth. Although they were true. The woman next to him was becoming more important than a business deal. That was undeniable.

Her eyes widened. "You'd lose millions of dollars, maybe more."

He gave a short nod. "I know."

She leaned over and kissed his cheek, then pulled back. "You do what you are good at, and I'm sure my grandma and sister will be only too happy to keep you in line. As for me, I trust you."

If Nick hadn't been driving, he would have pulled her into a fierce kiss.

19

IN ANY OTHER case, Lauren would have called her date off and phoned her grandmother or Sofia. She couldn't believe that Sofia had predicted Nick's counteroffer. Yeah, Nick *was* different, but where was the line drawn between business and relationships? Lauren honestly didn't know anymore. But she'd come to learn that first impressions could be way, way off-base. And Nick was the perfect example of that.

As they sped along the San Diego freeway, headed north, his warm hand cradling hers, she felt something she hadn't ever with another man. Comfortable. Content. Yes, the future was unknown, vastly so, yet . . . Right here, right now, being with Nick was where she wanted to be.

Even if they were about to see his mother.

Lauren had rarely met the parents of any man she'd dated, but Nick was different. He knew her background, the *real* her, and so dating him felt more real. More scary, truth be told.

But she didn't want to let go of his hand. She wanted this drive to last for hours. She wanted him to kiss her again.

"What are you thinking about, sweetheart?" Nick asked.

"Isn't that the woman's line?" She was stalling, trying to come up with something that wasn't what she'd been actually thinking about. She was also trying not to let the way that Nick called her *sweetheart* go to her head. He'd said it once before, just before he kissed her for the first time.

Nick squeezed her hand. "Is there a rule book somewhere that I don't know about?"

"*Men are from Mars, Women are from Venus*?"

He chuckled. "That's a book I've never read."

Lauren peeked at him, appreciating the way his dark hair nearly touched his collar and how he hadn't shaved today, giving him a bit of scruff along his chin. "Well, you should. You'll then clearly understand the differences between men and women."

His hazel eyes flicked to hers. "I've never had a problem noticing how a woman is different than me." His voice was low, and goose bumps broke out on her arms. "And I think you're avoiding the question."

"You know," Lauren said, still hedging, "sometimes thoughts are private, and they should stay that way."

"I agree," he said. "But that doesn't mean I can't ask you and hope you'll answer. Unless it's something like plotting my imminent demise because you're secretly furious that I'll be partnering with Ambrose Oil."

She couldn't help laughing. "You should have been a writer," she said. "You've got a great imagination."

"You're still stalling," Nick said, his lips quirking. "Will it be in the library with the candlestick?"

Lauren scoffed. "More like the conservatory with the wrench."

"Ouch," Nick said. "Remind me not to wander a giant mansion with you."

"Like Ambrose?"

"I'd be fine at Ambrose," he said. "I think your grandma would stand up for me, and besides, it's beautiful there."

Lauren felt inordinately pleased he'd complimented her childhood home. "Okay, Mr. Matthews, if you really want to know what I was thinking about . . . it was how I liked your kissing."

Nick didn't say anything, didn't even seem to react, but a few moments later he pulled off the next exit. She was about to ask him where they were going, but then she saw a sign for a museum.

Nick didn't head for the museum, though, and instead pulled to the side of the road as soon as they were off the freeway.

Lauren couldn't figure out why he was stopping. Then he released her hand and lifted his to her shoulder. She looked over at him, only to witness the intensity in his gaze.

His thumb brushed against her neck as his gaze dropped to her mouth. Predictably, her stomach erupted in butterflies.

"You can't say things like that and expect me to not act on it," he said in a quiet voice.

Then he leaned toward her and brushed his mouth against hers.

She loved the softness of his lips, the way he smelled, the way he ran his fingers along her neck, then slid his hand behind her neck to draw her closer.

Lauren moved her hand to his arm and tilted her head and let him take the kiss deeper. His other hand rested on her thigh, and she could feel the heat of his hand through the fabric of her dress. The way he kissed her told her more than words could. He liked her, a lot, and she already felt the same way.

When he broke off after a breathless few moments, he leaned his forehead against hers. "What else were you thinking about?"

She heard the smile in his voice, and she couldn't help the tingle of happiness that traveled the length of her body. "I think I've shared enough of my thoughts."

He chuckled, then kissed the edge of her jaw, lingering.

She traced her hand along his cheek, then down his neck, and rested it on the shoulder that was solid beneath his shirt.

"I like your kissing too, sweetheart," he whispered.

Butterflies zoomed through her, and she was pretty sure by the way her skin had heated that she was blushing. "Thank you, I guess."

He chuckled, then kissed the spot on her neck right below her ear, and the bristle of his chin softly scraped hers. More goose bumps. "As tempting as you are, we have an agenda, you know."

"Oh, what's that?" she murmured.

He kissed a little farther down her neck. "There's a museum I want to show you."

She ran her hand down his arm, then drew back. "Okay, let's go."

Nick lifted his head. "Just like that?"

"Well, we don't want to be late to your mother's function."

His gaze searched hers, and something in his eyes made warmth pool in her belly. She gently pushed him away. "Drive, Romeo."

He shook his head, smiling. After checking for traffic, he pulled onto the road again.

As they turned into the parking lot of the museum, Lauren read the sign aloud: "*The Museum of Making Music.*"

"Have you ever been?" he asked.

"No. Sounds interesting, though," she said as he pulled into a parking stall. Only a handful of cars were in the lot.

"I thought you might like it, since you listen to all the old stuff."

Yeah. Nick was all right.

He opened his door, then said, "Wait for me."

So she waited for him to walk around the car and open her door. *More than all right.* He held out his hand to help her to her feet. Not that she needed the help, but the chivalry was nice. Besides, he didn't let go of her hand, and she wasn't about to complain about that.

As they walked to the museum entrance, Nick said, "Did I tell you that you look beautiful?"

Lauren flashed him a smile. "I don't remember."

He stopped and pulled her against him, locking her in his arms.

She laughed and pushed against chest. "Okay, I remember, and yes, you did tell me. Thank you." Then she rose up on her toes and kissed his cheek. "You need to behave, Mr. Matthews."

She drew away, and he groaned, which only made her laugh again. They reached the entrance, holding hands again, and Nick paid for their admission into the museum.

They spent the next hour walking through the exhibits, learning about the history of musical instruments and everything from manufacturing the instruments to distribution and marketing. It seemed that Nick was well familiar with the place, but he gave Lauren time to soak everything in.

When they stopped at the innovation station, where patrons could play musical instruments for themselves, Nick pulled out a stool by a set of guitars. "Have a seat."

She sat, and he took his place on the opposite stool, then picked up one of the guitars.

"Don't tell me you play," she said.

He flashed a smile. "A little. You know, high school stuff like every wannabe kid."

But when he picked out a tune, Lauren was mesmerized. He was much better than a wannabe high school kid. "Is there anything you *can't* do, Nicholas Matthews?"

He lifted his gaze from the guitar. "I can't paint."

She smirked. "So there's *one* thing you can't do."

"Here," he said, rising to his feet and crossing to her. He set the guitar in her hands. "It's not hard." He helped her get her fingers in the right position. Then he guided her hands until she was playing a series of repetitive chords.

After she got the hang of the short melody, he sat on the stool across from her and folded his arms, a smile on his face. "Sounds great. The museum might hire you for demos."

"Funny," Lauren said, although she was enjoying playing what Nick had taught her. "My fingers are getting a workout." She lifted her left hand and looked at the indentations on the pads of her fingers.

"I think you'll live." Nick was on his feet again, and he took her hand in his and kissed each fingertip.

Lauren's skin buzzed. The museum wasn't crowded, but they were definitely in public. "You're not what I expected," she said in a quiet voice.

His hazel eyes scanned her face. "What did you expect?"

She pulled her hand from his and set the guitar back in its place, where they'd found it. She felt Nick watching her, and when she turned, he was still waiting.

She kept her voice low as another couple arrived at the innovation center. "I don't want to make your head too big."

One of his brows lifted. "I think I can handle it."

"Come on," she said, grasping his hand, liking how it was becoming so easy to touch him. And how natural and comfortable it felt. He let her lead him out of the museum.

He also let her lead him to the car, but when he opened her door, he slid his arm around her waist. "I want to know what you expected."

She lifted her chin to meet his eyes. Why did he have to be so good-looking? He definitely had more than his fair share of everything the world had to offer. "Well... when I first saw you and what you were wearing and your whole demeanor, I knew you were one of those wealthy guys. And I guess I assumed that you fit the usual profile."

"Like what...?"

"You know, full of your own self-importance. Basically, a jerk."

"Ouch." He moved his other hand to her waist so he was holding her in a loose embrace. "You know, having money doesn't automatically make someone a jerk."

She gave a small nod. "But instead, you were thoughtful and noticed the small things around you. Which I should have guessed when you offered to share your taxi when we first met at the airport. And then other stuff, like this museum."

His gaze was completely focused on her. "Maybe I'm just making excuses to be with you."

She rested her hands on his biceps. "You've negotiated with my grandmother in her favor."

"I'm not a business tyrant," he said with a wink. "At least not most of the time."

"You put me up when Kevin was being a creep," she said.

"He's still a creep," Nick said, an edge to his voice.

"And you like my art; at least, you *act* like it."

Nick leaned down and whispered in her ear, "I love your art."

She smiled as he pressed a kiss against her thrumming skin. She ran her fingers over the scruff of his jaw as he lingered. The butterflies in her stomach refused to calm down. "Maybe next time I can give you a discount."

He chuckled.

"Okay, Romeo, we're making a scene," she said as another car turned into the parking lot. She reluctantly moved away from him and slid into her seat.

As Nick walked around the front of the car, Lauren pulled out her cell phone and texted her sister Sofia. *You were right. I'm in trouble. Aka Nick Matthews.*

20

STRANDS OF WHITE lights twinkled around the topiary trees at the entrance of the gala event. Soft music floated out of the building as Nick grasped Lauren's hand while they walked through the entrance together. He hadn't told her that Chelsey would be here, but Lauren would likely find out soon enough. There'd never been anything between him and Chelsey, and Nick was quite sure she wasn't as brokenhearted as their mothers seemed to think.

Lauren wouldn't have to worry in the least, because Nick was feeling things for her he hadn't felt for any other woman. He couldn't exactly pinpoint the moment that he'd started to look at Lauren as someone other than a beautiful and interesting woman—which she still was, but now he wanted this date to be the first of many, and the first of many things.

But knowing that Lauren had never allowed herself to be in a serious relationship, one with a future in mind, told Nick that he'd have to take things at her pace. No matter how involved his heart already was.

"Nicholas!" a woman called out.

The voice could be none other than his mother's.

Nick turned toward the adjoining hallway, and sure enough, there was his mother. With her expertly coiffed dark hair that would never see a day of gray to her long, shimmery silver gown, along with her dripping diamonds, she was the epitome of a woman who loved to wear her wealth.

"Mother," he said, crossing to her, still holding Lauren's hand.

He released Lauren to kiss his mother's cheek, and she gave him a tight-lipped smile.

"Did you bring her?" she asked under her breath.

"If you're referring to Lauren Ambrose, yes, I'd like to introduce you." Nick turned to Lauren, who was right next to him, hearing everything. "Lauren, this is my mother, Penny Matthews."

His mother held out her hand, and Lauren shook it.

"Nice to meet you, Mrs. Matthews," Lauren said.

"Oh, call me Penny," she said. "*Mrs.* sounds so formal and stuffy."

Nick wanted to laugh, because his mother was precisely that.

"Well, I wish I had time to get to know you, Lauren, but I've a gala to run," she said, her gaze effectively dismissing Lauren, then cutting to Nick with a *we'll talk later* expression.

As his mother waltzed away to greet more arrivals, Nick took hold of Lauren's hand again. "Sorry about that," he said in a quiet voice.

Lauren gave him a small smile. "You did warn me."

"Yeah, but that still doesn't excuse her rudeness."

"She loves her son and is protective."

"Did you really just say that?" Nick asked, his lips twisting in amusement. "I mean, that's an even worse excuse."

Lauren moved slightly closer to him. "It's not true?"

"I suppose it's true," he said, looking into her blue eyes. "But she more likely has her own agenda."

"Like Chelsey."

Nick was surprised, but maybe he shouldn't be. "Yeah, how did you know?"

"I'm an observant person," Lauren said with a smirk. "Remember, I have the artist's eye. I'm pretty sure the blond woman staring you down is Chelsey."

Nick could almost feel the shift in the air as he turned to see whom Lauren was talking about. It had to be Chelsey. And he was right.

Chelsey's cheeks were flushed pink and her eyes a little too bright, which probably meant she'd already gotten hold of the champagne. Nick could safely bet that the champagne flute in her hand was not her first of the night, no matter how early it was. She wobbled on her stilettos but caught her balance before stumbling into the group of people she was passing.

"Nick, darling," she crooned.

Now, Nick knew Chelsey used endearments without any real meaning. He just hoped that Lauren wouldn't get offended.

"Chelsey," Nick said. "Nice to see you."

She grinned as she continued walking right up to him. Then she leaned in for a kiss, on the mouth. Nick dodged the kiss and awkwardly patted her shoulder.

Chelsey drew back and pushed her lips into a pout. "Baby, you're not happy to see me?"

"Chelsey," Nick cut in. "This is Lauren. My date."

Chelsey took some effort to swing her gaze over to Lauren. Chelsey also made no secret of scanning Lauren from head to toe. "She's pretty. Where'd you find her?"

Nick grimaced, and as the waiter walked past with a tray of champagne, Nick took the glass from Chelsey's hand and set it on the tray.

"Wait, that was mine," Chelsey said.

"I didn't want you to drop it," Nick deadpanned as she swayed on her feet.

"Oh, good idea," she said. "I am feeling a little dizzy."

"Here, why don't you sit down?" He grasped her arm and led her to a chair in the corner of the lobby. Before he could release her, she tried to pull him down with her.

Nick drew back firmly, but he still had to pry one of her hands from his arm. "You sit here until you feel better."

"Where are you going?" Chelsey said, her eyes glistening with . . . *tears*? Oh boy.

"I'm taking my date into the gala so we can bid on some items."

"Oh," Chelsey said, biting her lip, then sighing. "She seems nice. Is she nice?"

Nick couldn't imagine what Lauren thought of all of this. "Yes, she's nice. I'll see you a little later on."

"Okay," Chelsey said, closing her eyes.

Nick stepped away, then turned to find Lauren.

She was waiting where he'd left her. She stood with her arms folded, looking decidedly uncomfortable, and Nick didn't blame her. Out of the two women she'd met, one had been rude and dismissive, the other drunk.

"Sorry about that," he said.

Both of them watched Nick's mom walk over to Chelsey and try to help her to her feet.

Lauren narrowed her eyes. Before she could say anything, Nick said, "I'm going to bid on a few things, and then we can get out of here. Maybe this wasn't such a good idea."

"Is Chelsey normally like this?" Lauren asked.

"Not so early in the evening," Nick said. "But she definitely likes to party. Come on." He grasped her hand.

They walked into the banquet room, and together they browsed through silent-auction items. "Do you see anything you like?" Nick asked.

"Not really," Lauren said. "I'm not much of a stuff collector." She paused by an offer of music lessons by a violin master. "And I think I'm too old to take violin."

Nick stepped closer to her, appreciating her wildflower scent. "It's never too late to follow your dreams."

"Ha." Lauren didn't seem to mind his nearness. "I don't think being a musician has ever been my dream, although I do enjoy playing."

He slid his other hand to her waist, appreciating the soft fabric of her dress. "So, what is your dream, Lauren Ambrose?"

"To have my art at the Metropolitan Museum."

Nick stilled. "Which one?"

"New York, of course."

He felt a smile grow within him. "My father's cousin is the curator."

Lauren spun around to face him, her blue eyes stunned. "No."

He chuckled. "Yes."

"Wow." She stared at him for a moment, and he waited for her to ask . . .

But she didn't ask. "That's a coincidence."

Nick leaned down. "Definitely."

She pursed her lips, her eyes shining, and she tugged his hand to another display. "The Greek Island Spa Giveaway. The one thing you should never live without."

"Want it?" Nick said in a quiet voice.

"The starting bid is twenty thousand."

Nick shrugged. "Do you want it?"

She turned to look up at him. "You're a nut. Besides, I can totally live without a Greek Island Spa Getaway. I've been surviving fine for thirty years."

Nick considered her. "What couldn't you live without, Lauren Ambrose?"

She didn't answer at first but led him to the next display. A Hawaii vacation for two. "Um, I'm not sure I should say. You'd probably think *I'm* nuts."

"Tell me," Nick urged. He simply wanted to know as much about her as he could.

"So, I'm a pretty frugal person, but there's one splurge I made a few years ago."

Nick waited, watching and loving the soft smile on her face.

"I bought a Renoir painting," she said.

Nick blinked. He wasn't an expert on the price of art, but he was pretty sure a Renoir piece would be hundreds of thousands of dollars. "Which one?" Again, he didn't know if he'd recognize the name, but he was curious.

She pulled out her cell phone and opened her photo app, then showed him a picture of a painting of roses. "*Roses dans un vase de fleurs*," she said.

"Wow," Nick said. "Where do you keep it?"

"In a safe place that's not easily accessible."

He raised his brows. "Not your condo, I hope."

"No." She moved closer, which he didn't mind at all. "It's in the locked safe of the gallery. I look at it from time to time; otherwise, the picture on my phone will have to do."

"Maybe you should make a replica," he suggested.

At Lauren's furrowed brow, he knew he'd suggested wrong.

"Renoir could never be duplicated," she said. "And to try to do so would be wrong."

Nick nodded. "I get that. I mean, *you* could never be duplicated either."

She smirked, and he leaned down and kissed her right beneath her earlobe.

"Have we been here long enough?" he whispered.

Lauren rested a hand against his chest, which only sent his heart into overdrive. "Ask your mother if it's okay to go, and then we'll head out."

Nick groaned, and Lauren smiled.

"I don't want her hating me more than she already does," Lauren said. "She might think I'm dragging you away."

"She doesn't hate you," Nick said. "She's a very self-involved woman, and she doesn't always see beyond the surface of other people."

"Speaking of . . ."

Nick turned to see Chelsey walking toward them, a sloppy smile on her face. *Oh no.*

"There you are, Nicky boy," Chelsey said, stopping next to him, and nearly tipping against him. "I've been looking for you."

"You should really sit down," Nick said. "You don't look so well."

Chelsey patted her hair, then ran a hand over her face. "What's wrong? Is my mascara smeared?"

Nick had no words.

"Here you are," Lauren said, guiding Chelsey with a firm grip past the auction table to the nearest gala table. "This is your place, and you shouldn't move until Nick tells you to."

Chelsey's eyes rounded as she sat on one of the banquet chairs. "Oh, okay. Who are you?"

"I'm Lauren," she said simply. "Remember to stay here. It's very important."

Chelsey gave an enthusiastic nod.

Lauren returned to Nick's side. "Maybe we should skip out early."

The gala room was becoming more crowded, and people milled about, signing up for the silent auction, and Nick was dreading the rest of the evening with a drunk Chelsey and a hostile mother. "Sounds good to me. Let's stop by the pledge table first, and then I think we can escape through a side door without my mom noticing."

"Your mom noticing what?" a woman said, startling them both.

Nick gritted his teeth, then put on a smile and turned. "Hi, Mom. I was going to make a cash donation, because I'm not interested in any of the auction items."

His mother covered up her cool look with a smile. "That would be fine, dear. Did you see Chelsey sitting by herself? You should go talk to her."

His mom completely ignored Lauren, and it bothered Nick to no end.

He lowered his voice. "Chelsey's drunk. She needs to sleep it off. And like I said, Lauren's my date tonight."

His mother lifted her chin. "You're in a snippy mood tonight."

It took all of his willpower not to respond to her accusation. "I'll see you later," he said in a calm tone. "I'm headed to the pledge table now."

His mother's gaze appraised him and only him. "Don't be stingy like your father."

Nick was out of patience. He grasped Lauren's hand and drew her with him to the pledge table. He signed his name to a $5,000 pledge, then turned to Lauren. "Let's go."

21

Lauren fought to keep her heart rate calm as she followed Nick out of the building. It was clear he was upset with his mother, and she didn't blame him. As for herself, Lauren had decided not to take the woman's insults personally. There was a reason Lauren kept mostly to herself and stayed away from people who thought they could buy their way into anything and bully anyone in the process.

Mrs. Matthews was a product of her world, for better or for worse. Too bad she was Nick's mom.

Nick led her by the hand, which he was gripping rather tightly, to the valet stand, where Nick requested his car to be returned.

Lauren hadn't been around Nick before when he was angry, and although he wasn't saying much, she could practically see the steam rolling off his shoulders.

The car was brought around, and the valet climbed out. Nick handed him a twenty dollar bill and said, "Thank you."

His tone was clipped, though, and the valet nodded, then quickly got out of the way.

Surprisingly, Nick's touch was gentle on her back as he guided her to the car and opened the passenger door for her. As she waited for him to walk around the front of the car, her mind reeled with all that had happened, but it only solidified her resolve to stay away from wealthy people in general, especially drunk wealthy people.

On one hand, she felt a little sorry for Nick if his mother was the prime example of a woman in his life. And what mother would try to set up her son with someone like Chelsey? Granted, she was probably a little different when *not* intoxicated, but still, it was baffling. Was control of money really that important to his mother? To sacrifice her son's happiness and ignore his wishes?

When he got inside the car, he said, "Ready?"

His tone wasn't as hard, but after she nodded, he pulled out of the parking lot a little fast. Okay, really fast, and Lauren found herself gripping the seat. They drove in silence for several moments, and she wondered if they'd make the entire two-hour drive without speaking. She definitely wasn't going to start the conversation.

When red and blue lights flashed behind them, Nick cursed and slowed down, then pulled over to the shoulder of the road. They hadn't even made it to the freeway yet.

An officer approached his side of the car, and after getting the registration and insurance information, the cop issued a speeding citation.

If Lauren hadn't felt numb about everything, she might have found it ironic and even funny. As it was, Nick was still pretty grim, and when the officer left, he tucked the ticket into the jockey box, then pulled onto the main road again.

It wasn't until they were on the freeway that he spoke.

"I'm sorry about my mom," he said, his tone sounding defeated. "She's . . . she has a lot of issues, none of them having to do with you, and yet she treated you horribly."

His left hand was gripping the steering wheel, and his right hand was resting on his thigh, so Lauren reached over and took his hand. "She's scared about her future."

Nick turned his gaze to her, his brows furrowed. "What do you mean, *scared*? She's a wealthy woman, regardless of the shared trust."

"She lost a husband," Lauren began.

"Ex."

"*Ex*-husband," Lauren said. "She sees any woman you date as a threat because she'll no longer be the number-one woman in your life."

Nick scoffed. Then his expression relaxed. "You really think that's what she feels?"

"Yes," Lauren said in a soft tone. "She's lashing out, trying to keep her control in whatever way possible. But she doesn't realize she's only pushing you away."

Nick nodded. "Exactly." He intertwined their fingers. "You're an amazing woman, Lauren Ambrose. And understanding. And sweet. You're beautiful, intelligent, talented. And too good for my mother, and probably me—"

"Stop," Lauren said with a laugh. "I'm not that amazing." She loved that Nick's mouth turned up at the corners. His brooding seemed to be over, and hopefully the anger gone. Yeah, it was justified, but Lauren also recognized that beneath the glittery and aloof exterior of Penny Matthews was a woman who loved her son.

His gaze was on her again, and although the night was dark, she felt the intensity all the same. "You are amazing. If I say so, then it's true. I don't lie, Lauren, so I'd appreciate if you'd learn to take a compliment." His wink drove heat straight to her belly.

From there, warmth spread to the rest of her body. "Well, thank you, sir. You're kind of amazing yourself."

He was still gazing at her, and well, he was still driving.

"Eyes on the road, Romeo."

Nick looked at the road, but seconds later, she felt his gaze on her again, and she squeezed his hand. He squeezed back.

Raindrops began to fall in single increments, then more and more, until Nick had to turn on the wiper blades.

The silence between them was comfortable now, even companionable. The rain fell in earnest, but Nick didn't have a problem driving through it. Lauren loved that about him. His confidence. His way of getting things done. How he held her hand like he wasn't planning on letting go anytime soon.

And . . . she had so many questions, mostly because she knew her heart was getting caught up in this man beside her. She was curious. She wanted to know more. She wanted to know everything.

By the time they reached her place, Lauren was feeling sleepy, but in a good way. Like she could fall asleep in no time with a smile on her face. The rain hadn't let up when they'd parked, and Nick reached behind the seat, searching for something.

Then he clicked on the overhead dome light, and Lauren blinked in the light.

"What are you looking for?" she asked.

"Umbrella."

"You afraid of a little rain?"

He met her gaze. "No . . ."

She grinned, then popped open her door. "Coming?" she asked before climbing out.

He called her name, but she shut the door and ran to her condo. She was shivering and nearly soaked by the time she arrived.

Nick was right behind her. "You're crazy," he panted as she unlocked the door with a shiver.

She grabbed the front of his shirt and pulled him into her dark apartment. Then they were kissing. Despite the fact that Lauren was cold and wet, she was soon warmed by Nick's mouth on hers and his hands cradling her face.

She blindly shut the door, and he moved her against it, so that she was trapped between the door and his body. Which she didn't mind in the least.

Nick's kissing slowed and turned more exploratory, more methodical, which only raised Lauren's pulse several notches. This man had the ability to stir all of her senses to life with one kiss and send her into a place of sweet oblivion.

His phone buzzed, but he ignored it.

Then Lauren realized it was her phone. And she still ignored it.

Nick drew away, his breathing heavy. "Do you need to answer your phone?"

"No." She exhaled. "Don't stop kissing me."

His chuckle was low, but his next kiss was soft, then he rested his forehead against hers. "You're shivering."

"It's a good shiver," she said.

This time Nick kissed her again, properly. She moved her hands over his shoulders and around his warm neck. She was infatuated with this man, that she knew, and as she pulled him closer, she thought of how hard it would be to let him go. Her phone rang again.

"Lauren, it's nearly midnight," he whispered against her skin.

The thought sent a jolt through her. No good calls came at midnight. She reached for her phone, and Nick stepped away to flip on a light.

"Sofia?" she answered.

"I've been trying to get hold of you for hours," Sofia said. "Why aren't you answering?"

Lauren moved the phone and looked at her call log. Sure enough, there were several missed calls, but she hadn't heard the phone ring. "My phone must have been out of service," she said, panic building. "What's wrong? Is it Grandma?"

"Granny's fine," Sofia said, then took a breath. "I was calling about something I needed to run past you. And when you didn't answer your phone or call me back for a few hours, I started to worry."

Lauren moved to the kitchen and sat on a chair since she didn't want to get the couch damp. Nick stayed standing, his arms folded.

"How much time have you been spending with Nicholas Matthews?" Sofia asked.

This was not what Lauren expected. "Why?"

Sofia let out a sigh. "Are you with him right now?"

Lauren glanced at Nick.

"Hi, Sofia," he said in a clear tone.

"Put me on speaker, then," Sofia said.

So, Lauren did, and Nick came to sit at the table too.

"Hi, Sofia," Nick said. "Nice to hear from you."

Sofia released a half laugh. "She knows, right?"

"Yes." Nick's gaze met Lauren's. "Do you have any updates?" he asked Sofia.

"I do," Sofia said. "Our grandmother is planning on signing tomorrow. All terms are agreeable."

Lauren stared at Nick. The triumph in his eyes was unmistakable. "Great," he said. "Do you have any concerns?"

"You've been good enough to address most of them so far," Sofia said. "I do have one more concern, though—which I was going to talk to Lauren about—but I might as well speak to both of you at the same time."

Lauren rested her hands on the table, clasping them tightly.

"Shoot," Nick said, his gaze still locked with Lauren's.

"I need to show you something in person."

Lauren knew immediately what Sofia was speaking about. "No, Sofia," she said. "Don't bother. It's not going to work."

"I'm proof that the curse can be broken," Sofia said. "So is Gavin."

Lauren dropped her head. "You don't know that," she said in a quiet voice. "You *can't* know that. Not yet."

"I do know it, Lauren," Sofia said. "I feel different now. And you will too. You'll know when the curse is broken for yourself." Her voice dropped. "The fear is gone. Completely gone. I can't tell you how freeing it's been. Besides, if you believe in the curse, then you can believe it will be broken."

Lauren closed her eyes and rubbed her temples.

"Nick might as well deliver the paperwork himself, and you can come with him," Sofia said. "Let Nick read Margaret Ambrose's journal for himself, and then he can decide. That's what I did with Gavin."

Lauren lowered her hands. "It's not like that between us . . . I mean . . . We . . ." Her words were getting jumbled, and by the frown on Nick's face, she knew that he was confused too.

"I can deliver the paperwork in person, no problem," Nick said. "Does Wednesday work?"

"Yes," Sofia said. "Both of you can stay here. We have plenty of room. Thanks, Nick. And Lauren, call me later—tomorrow morning preferably."

Before Lauren could agree or disagree, Sofia had hung up.

Lauren closed her eyes again, knowing that Nick would want an explanation. And he deserved one. Then she opened her eyes and narrowed them. "Have you and Sofia been talking about . . . me?"

"*Us*," Nick said. "I might have told her we were, uh, dating." The question in his eyes made her feel his vulnerability—something that Lauren hadn't seen in him before. It was kind of . . . endearing.

"You mean this entire time I've been cryptic with my sister about . . . us . . . she already knew." The slight dip of his chin confirmed it. "She must have been laughing at me."

Nick set his hand over her folded ones. "Well, I don't want to get in the middle of your relationship with your sister, but she said you're like a locked box when it comes to sharing your life with her."

That was true. "You just said you didn't want to come between us."

He leaned forward, those hazel eyes on her. "Come with me to Ambrose," he said in a low voice. "Your sister told me about your second-great-grandmother's journal. I want to read it."

Lauren's heart pounded for a lot of reasons, namely because letting Nick read the journal was giving him more access to her life and to the growing feelings for him that she was trying hard to tamp down.

"Why?" she said. "Why do you want to read the journal?"

"Because I was hoping to find a way to help you break the curse that has you living in fear every moment of your life."

She blew out a breath. Despite the stinging in her eyes, she refused to let any tears fall. "I'm fine," she said, but her voice trembled. "I've been fine for thirty years."

Nick rubbed his thumb over her hand, and Lauren loved how his touch could make her feel immediately comforted. She also hated that he could have such a powerful effect on her emotions.

"Don't you want to see if there can be more?" he asked in a soft voice. "A future that's less lonely?"

She blinked.

Nick lifted his hand and brushed his fingertips along her jaw. "Let me in, Lauren Ambrose. Take a chance."

"Why?" she whispered.

"Because I can see myself falling in love with you, sweetheart," he said, "And I don't want to lose you."

Lauren's body stilled, but her mind raced as his words rocketed through her.

"I don't know, Nick," she finally said. "I guess I am afraid."

22

"You've never flown first class?" Nick asked as he looked over at Lauren with surprise.

She rolled her carry-on ahead of him, in a hurry, it seemed, although first-class passengers had priority boarding.

"No," she said. "I always thought it was . . . pretentious."

Finally she slowed her step, looking a little chagrined at the comment.

Nick didn't mind. He wanted to hear all of Lauren's thoughts, good or bad. It was Wednesday, and since that phone call with Sofia on Sunday night, Lauren had been . . . edgy. For lack of a better word. He'd taken her out to dinner on Monday night, but Lauren's conversation had been distracted.

Yet Nick took heart that she *was* traveling to Ambrose with him. Despite the fact that he'd nearly told her he was in love with her, and she hadn't returned the sentiment. Lauren was a juxtaposition of emotions, it seemed. She had closed herself off to substantial relationships her entire life. She rarely spoke to her grandmother and even less to her other sisters. And with Sofia, she seemed to be carrying the weight of the relationship between the two sisters.

Not that Nick's relationship with either of his parents was perfect. He hadn't fully appreciated his father until the last year of his life. And his mom—their relationship was shallow at best. Despite Lauren's hang-ups and reservations, Nick only wanted to crack through them more and discover the real Lauren.

Following their dinner on Monday night, she'd taken him to the gallery, where Freddie had let them in after hours. Together, the three of them had stood before the Renoir for at least thirty minutes, just staring at it.

Lauren had been right. The piece was magnificent, almost holy.

And Nick had been speechless. Lauren had reached for his hand, and as their fingers linked, he knew that this woman who felt so much and had sacrificed so much had his heart in her hands.

At her doorstep after, she'd given him a fierce hug but no kiss, and she had seemed anxious to get inside her condo.

Now, Lauren moved down the aisle of the plane in front of him, and before she could load her carry-on in the overhead compartment, he grasped it from her.

"I've got it," he said.

She nodded, and when both of their bags were tucked away, he sat next to her.

Lauren stared out the window into the drippy morning. The rain was gentle, and wouldn't cause any issues with taking off.

"You okay?" he asked, wrapping his hand over hers.

She nodded but said nothing, keeping her gaze trained on the window.

Nick held back a sigh, and it wasn't until they were in the air, the plane evened out, that he tried again. "What are you most worried about?"

She didn't answer for a moment, then she looked over at him. The sadness in her eyes made his stomach feel hollow.

"You."

He raised his brows. "*Me?* Why?"

"Why do you think?" she asked.

"Because . . . you think I'll die a tragic premature death?"

She blinked. "It's not funny."

He leaned close, only a breath apart from her beautiful face. "I'm not laughing, sweetheart." He kissed her lightly, not sure how she'd react.

His heart leapt as she lifted a hand and placed it behind his neck as she finally responded, kissing him back slowly and sweetly. When she pulled back, her cheeks were pink. "We're on a plane, Nick."

He exhaled. "I'm glad you're coming with me to Ambrose."

She bit her lip, which only made him want to kiss her again. But he'd have to settle for holding her hand.

"I don't know about this," she said in a quiet voice. "I mean . . . there's a cemetery full of—"

"I know." Nick slipped his arm around her shoulders and drew her close. He was gratified when she sighed and rested her head against his shoulder.

No, he didn't know the future, but if Lauren and her sisters believed in the power of a curse, then he'd do what he could to help her break it. He was definitely curious to know what the journal said, yet he didn't want to upset Lauren. He was treading as carefully as he could, letting her take the lead, but the truth was, he was in love with her. That he couldn't deny.

He'd already fallen. Already lost his heart.

And as the woman leaning against him closed her eyes and let him pull her closer, he knew there was nothing more important to him than making sure she was happy and protected. It was a surreal feeling, to be sure. Nicholas Matthews had finally lost his heart. His mother would find out soon enough, and he didn't know how much longer he could wait to tell Lauren, so for now, it would be his own secret.

He sensed that if he told Lauren too early, she'd backtrack in their relationship, possibly even breaking things off. It seemed to be her automatic response to things that got too complicated. The thing was, Nick didn't mind the complication. Yeah, there were a lot of layers to deal with here, and he sensed that there was even more to Lauren Ambrose than she'd let him glimpse. She was an intriguing woman.

When the plane landed, Nick rose to his feet and lifted down both of their luggage items, then he let Lauren lead the way off the plane. He'd rented a car, and he wasn't surprised that Lauren had little to say. She was back to her reflective mood.

Once they were in the car, heading to Ambrose, Lauren said, "I don't want to offend you or anything, but your, um, tendency toward PDA might be a little shocking for my grandmother."

Nick glanced over at Lauren. "You mean like kissing or like holding hands?"

"All of it." Her gaze connected with his. "It's just that things between us are new, and she's kind of old-fashioned, if you know what I mean."

"What about if we're alone in one of the dark hallways?" Nick teased.

"Then . . . maybe we could relax the rules a little."

"Good enough for me," he said, reaching for her hand.

Her fingers linked with his, and he found them cool to the touch. "Are you nervous?"

She nodded, and when he stopped at the traffic light headed into town, he leaned over and kissed the edge of her jaw.

"Like that," she said, sounding breathless. "You can't do that."

"We're not at Ambrose yet." And since the light was still red, he cradled her face and kissed her on the mouth.

He could feel her desire in her response, and he'd have to be satisfied with that for now. He didn't know if Lauren felt the same way about him as he did her. He could only hope. And wait.

Lauren drew away, her expression softer than it had been in days. "The light's green."

He pulled forward, his pulse jumping from the contact with Lauren. He couldn't get enough of her, and he wasn't too excited about keeping his hands to himself while at Ambrose. Hopefully there would be plenty of dark hallways.

When they arrived at the estate, they bypassed a construction truck. "What's going on?" he asked Lauren.

"I think Sofia has insisted on some upgrades and put one of my other sisters in charge," Lauren said. "I've stayed out of it."

Nick could see that about Lauren. She really didn't like complications or conflict, and her family had plenty of it. He parked to the side of the massive garage, not wanting to block anyone from coming and going, then he climbed out and opened the trunk of the car. After unloading the two bags, he looked over at Lauren. She stood, staring at the house, her arms folded.

Nick hid a sigh. He wished she'd be more open with him. Moving to her side, he said, "Everything okay?"

She met his gaze, a worried look in her eyes. "I didn't think I'd be back so soon."

Nick realized then that somehow Ambrose haunted her. He didn't think she hated the place, but she didn't seem to love it either. Maybe he could change her opinion, since it really was an amazing estate. Full of history and intrigue.

The front door opened before they could reach it, and Sofia stepped out. She wore an elegant business suit, and her smile was broad. Much different than when Nick had first met her. This Sofia was rather welcoming instead.

"I saw the car," Sofia said. "Although Shelton could have easily fetched you."

"Thanks for the offer." Nick stepped forward to shake her hand.

Sofia and Lauren gave each other a brief hug, and when they separated, Nick asked, "How's your grandmother?"

"She's ready for you," Sofia said, glancing at Lauren. "We'd like you in the meeting too."

"Of course." Lauren's tone was formal, almost clipped.

"Great," Sofia said. "I've got refreshments set up. I know what plane food is like."

Nick chuckled, but Lauren remained silent. She was stoic and beautiful, no matter that she wasn't as formally dressed as her sister. Lauren's long skirt and V-neck blouse set off her curves, and Nick had firsthand knowledge of how soft the fabric of her clothing was and how she smelled like wildflowers.

He wanted to smooth back the hair that wisped about her face, if only for an excuse to touch her. But there was too much tension radiating from her. Plus, he'd agreed, no PDA. And . . . he had a business deal to close. Which he really should be focusing on.

Sofia opened the door wide, and Nick carried in both suitcases. "Shelton will take those to your room for you."

And before Nick could protest, Shelton appeared and picked up the bags.

"This way," Sofia said. "We're meeting in the dining room for the table space." She headed down the wide corridor, and Nick and Lauren followed, walking beneath the crystal chandelier.

Mrs. Lillian Ambrose was sitting at the head of the dining table, looking as regal as a queen in her ivory suit and elegantly coiffed hair. Ruby earrings studded her ears, and she wore a diamond-and-ruby necklace.

Lauren crossed to her grandmother and kissed the woman on the cheek.

"How are you, dear?" her grandmother asked. "I was hoping you'd come."

"Here I am," Lauren said with a smile.

Mrs. Ambrose turned her twinkling blue eyes on Nick. "Thanks for coming all this way again, Mr. Matthews."

"Not a problem." He stepped forward to shake her hand. "Anything for my business partner."

Mrs. Ambrose's laughter was soft, and she again focused on Lauren. "Help yourself to any of the food, and have a seat."

They both did, and Nick sat closest to Mrs. Ambrose so that he could go over each line of the contract with her. As expected, she asked several questions, and Nick was able to answer them to her satisfaction. The last thing he wanted to do was to have to redo the contract and delay it even more. He'd lined up the tech company to start work in a week, and it would be tricky to reschedule everything.

"Very good," Mrs. Ambrose said at last. Her gaze shifted to Lauren. "Do you have any questions?"

"No, I think everything is laid out clearly," Lauren said.

"And what about you, Sofia?" Mrs. Ambrose asked her eldest granddaughter.

"I'm satisfied," Sofia said. "Like I told you, if you want this partnership, then I support it."

"Very well." Mrs. Ambrose tapped her fingers. "Now give me that pen, young man."

Nick smiled and handed over his pen. Mrs. Ambrose made a show of signing each line indicated with her flowery signature. No one else spoke, and when she finished, she turned to Sofia.

"Your turn, dear."

Sophia signed next, then Mrs. Ambrose said, "I think I'm about done in for the afternoon. Can you help me to my room, and we'll all meet again for dinner?"

"I'll help you," Lauren said, suddenly rising to her feet. She seemed in need of a break of some sort, so Nick said nothing as the two women left.

"So . . ." Sofia said in a soft voice. "Lauren seems pretty freaked out. What did you do to her?"

Nick shrugged. "Nothing."

"You can't fool me, Nicholas Matthews." Sofia folded her arms. "My sister might keep her cards close, but she can't hide the fact that she's rattled about something."

Nick steepled his fingers. "I might have told her that I'm falling in love with her and that I want to help her break the curse."

"Well, that will do it." Sofia pushed back her chair and rose to her feet. "Come on. I want to show you my grandmother's journal."

"What about Lauren?" he asked, standing as well.

"She'll know where to find us."

As they left the dining room, Sofia linked her arm through his. "I like you, Nick. And I think you're a good match for my sister; in fact, I know it. You need to understand something about her, though; when things get too . . . hard . . . she doesn't stick around. She'd rather shut people out than face conflict."

"Yeah, I've guessed that already," Nick said in a dry tone.

"But don't take it personally," Sofia continued. "I mean, you told her how you felt, and I believe she feels the same way."

This stopped Nick in his tracks, and he turned to look at Sofia. "How do you know?"

"I know my sister," Sofia said. "I can hear it in her voice, and the way she was watching you while you were going over the contract, even though she was pretending not to, told me all that I needed to know. My sister *wants* to love you. She *wants* to be with you. She just doesn't know how to give herself permission."

"So you're saying this goes deeper than the curse?"

Sofia hesitated, then nodded. "Part of breaking the curse is believing that we can live a full life with it no longer hanging over our heads. Not too easy."

"If you don't mind me asking, how did *you* do it?"

Sofia's smile lit her face. "Gavin made it easy." She shrugged. "He believed so wholeheartedly despite any of my doubts, and eventually, I did too. Only then did the curse break once and for all."

"What happened to let you know?"

Sofia's smile turned secretive. "That's between Gavin and me. But *you'll* know. There will be no doubt, believe me."

Nick nodded. He'd have to trust in Sofia's explanation, along with finding a way to get through Lauren's walls.

Sofia seemed to notice his internal battle, because she tugged him toward the sweeping staircase. "She's worth it, you'll see," she said in a hushed voice. "Just don't give up."

Nick didn't plan to.

23

LAUREN FOUND THEM in the library, sitting on the settee, the journal in Sofia's hand. She hadn't opened it yet, but it was only a matter of time. Ever since her conversation with Sofia on Sunday night, Lauren had known this would be inevitable. Well, maybe since she realized that she wanted Nicholas Matthews in her life for more than a handful of dates.

He and her sister appeared to be getting along fine, and her grandmother had also seemed to like him well enough. Lauren stepped into the room, and both of them looked up.

"How's Granny?" Sofia asked.

"She says she wants to rest for a while," Lauren answered.

Sofia nodded. "Come sit." She rose and handed over the journal.

Lauren took the book and sat next to Nick. She very well knew what was inside, but opening it was still a strange experience, knowing that the penmanship was that of her great-great-grandmother Margaret Florence Thorne Ambrose.

"I've marked the entries that are the most important," Sofia said. "What you need to know leading up to it is that our great-great-grandparents Margaret and George had two boys, Matty and James, and one daughter, Helen. Their neighbors, the Fontaines, were very close friends." She paused. "Too close, it ended up, because Mrs. Celeste Fontaine and George Ambrose had an affair. A baby boy was the result, but he died."

Lauren could only stare at Sofia as her sister continued the story. "Celeste Fontaine was heartbroken, and Margaret was heartbroken as well when she found out about the affair. But tragedy hadn't ended.

Both of Margaret's sons Matty and James were killed in freak accidents. They were only boys. Of course, both families were torn apart for different reasons, but it all stemmed from the affair. But then George wanted to reconcile with his wife. This sent Celeste into a vengeful frenzy, and she used a fortune teller name Madame Zelana to cast a spell over the Ambrose family."

Sofia nodded at the journal Lauren held. "Read the next entries aloud, and then if Nick has questions, he can ask them after."

Lauren swallowed against the lump in her throat, then began to read:

Life Recordings of Margaret Florence Thorne Ambrose
May 2, 1912
My hand is shaking badly as I write this. My eyes so blurry I fear I'm going blind. My limbs are weak. I have taken to my bed.

Celeste took her final revenge. Two weeks ago, after learning that George would not leave me once and for all to come to her, she cursed him so that I couldn't have him.

He died while rounding up cattle with the foreman. Kicked in the head by the sire bull in preparation for mating season with the cows. My husband has ranched for seventeen years, and he was accompanied by experienced ranch hands, no less. His accident is no coincidence.

George succumbed to death a day later after lying in a coma.
The doctor said he died of a brain hemorrhage.
In less than six months I have lost my husband and two sons. How will I ever cope—or survive out here all alone?

Lauren's eyes burned with emotion. No one in the room spoke; no one moved. The only sound was the methodical ticking of the grandfather clock as if to confirm that, yes, time did pass. Lauren took a deep breath before continuing with the next entry.

Life Recordings of Margaret Florence Thorne Ambrose
August 31, 1912
My brother, Lloyd, sent his dear wife across the Atlantic to be here with me for the summer. Victoria is so good, so kind. I have

grown very fond of my sister-in-law. She brought her lady's maid, Nellie, with her so she wouldn't be alone on the ocean voyage.

Nellie lifts everyone's spirits with her genuine kindness and laughter and sweet singing.

Over the last few months, Victoria tried to get me out walking in the gardens, but for most of the summer I sat on the veranda overlooking the estate in my mourning garb, just staring. Occasionally holding Helen who is getting too big for my lap. Actually, she was too big about three years ago, but I crave her closeness, her sweetness, even when she fights to run off and swing in the gardens, or play with the new kittens in the barns.

Will Celeste take her from me, too? I begged Victoria to take her back to England with her to save her, but Victoria laughs off my worries. I tried to tell her about Celeste and George and the dead infant and the ties with the loss of my sons, but she is convinced it's all in my imagination.

Only I know the truth. Because I now have proof of it in Celeste's own hand.

In June, Mr. Fontaine sold their ranch and left for San Francisco with his wife. To start over and begin again.

I have never been so glad to see someone gone.

But the wicked curse that Madame Zelana concocted for my family over the last year was never undone. The fortune-teller with her séances and mutterings from the underworld disappeared from the village of Ambrose in June. No one knows where she went, but Celeste was sure to give me a dire warning that the Ambrose Curse was in effect until someone could break it. She would not tell me how the curse was to be broken. But in July, after she and Mr. Fontaine were safely in San Francisco I received a letter from the woman. Enclosed was the curse in Madame Zelana's own hand. Directed by Celeste for our downfall. She never could have loved George if she didn't care that he died. She only wanted me to suffer for her losses. She could not bear to know that I would have my husband and sons, and she nothing.

Since I cannot stand to look at the curse for one more second, I will write the details in my own words so my progeny will know what to do to save future generations.

Madame Zelana stated that in retribution for the loss of Celeste's son with George, and his subsequent betrayal to her, every Ambrose son and father and brother will die. Every Ambrose daughter or woman who marries will also lose their husbands and sons. Arrogance would not save Ambrose Estate from the curse. Only George could have done that and he had not given in to Celeste. In the end, he shunned her by not running away with her.

These facts confirmed to me—too late—that George had finally broken all association with her. Something I never believed from my husband's own mouth. Because I was too distrustful.

Celeste was bitter and vengeful. She had allowed her own sins to blacken her soul. She didn't care what her bitter envy would do to George and his family, the man she professed to love.

This is not love.

This is wickedness at its deepest depth.

Madame Zelana states in her vile curse that the only way to break the hold of the curse is for every Ambrose women to willingly give up, or lose, something they dearly love. If they do not, they too will lose the men they love.

The curse was written by Madame Zelana's own hand and signed with Celeste's own blood. The devil is in the details.

I am putting this Journal and Celeste's Curse in my trunk of mourning clothes. Helen is too young to be told these things yet, but before she is married, I will tell her.

I have vowed to do my part. I will not return to England. I will stay here and run the ranch and estate myself. All those hours of contemplation in the gardens and ruminating on the veranda of the house George and I built together convinced me that I belong here. England holds nothing for me any longer. It has been nearly twenty years, and it would be too difficult to start over.

George worked hard for this estate with my own dowry, and it's the only way I can honor his memory and have peace within myself.

May God bless my sweet Helen and all the future generations of granddaughters so Ambrose Estate will live on.

Be brave, Women of Ambrose Estate.

Lauren wiped at her eyes. She hadn't realized she'd been crying until the pages blurred before her. "So, the only way to break the curse is to give up something we love." She met Sofia's somber gaze. "Or lose it?"

Sofia gave a somber nod.

Lauren could feel Nick's gaze on her. But it was hard to look at him, because she knew he'd see the truth in her eyes—the truth that *he* was the one whom she loved and that *he* was the one she'd have to make a sacrifice for.

Sofia murmured something about giving them some time to themselves and left the room. Even with her gone, Lauren still couldn't look at Nick.

"Lauren," he whispered. Then his hand slid over hers. "What possession do you value the most?"

Her throat ached, and her eyes burned with tears.

Finally, she looked into those hazel eyes of his.

He nodded. "I think any man would be a fool to ask you to give up your Renoir."

The tears did spill onto her cheeks then. She knew it was ridiculous to put so much value into a painting from decades ago. But she loved it since it was hers and hers alone. The painting represented how she tried to live her life, in her own way and not catering to the world at large. How could Nick be so understanding of this? Surely he must know how she felt about him. She couldn't stop thinking about him for even one moment, and—

"I'm going to fly out tonight instead of tomorrow." Nick's words brought her into sharp focus.

"Wait, what?" she said in a thin voice.

"I think it's best, Lauren," he said, smiling.

The smile was sad, though, and that only made Lauren's heart ache more.

"How about you give me the grand tour of this place," he continued. "Then I'll head out. The contract's signed, your grandmother seems satisfied, and I don't want to wear out my welcome."

Lauren brushed at her cheeks and took a stuttering breath. Was

Nick *dumping* her? That was *her* job. Yet . . .

He rose to his feet and straightened that infernal tie he'd been wearing all day. He held out his hand. "How about that tour?"

Lauren looked at his hand. She knew it wasn't the affection she was hoping for but more of a conciliatory gesture. Despite her better judgment, she placed her hand in his, and as they passed by the bookcases, she set the journal atop a stack of books. Sofia would find it easily enough later. Or not. Lauren didn't care much for a decades-old curse that had only brought havoc and heartache to her life.

Nick was still holding her hand, but it wasn't like it used to be. Warm shivers weren't racing up and down her arms. A heaviness had settled in her chest, and her throat was aching again. Still, because she seemed to like being tortured, she walked with Nick through the main rooms of the house.

She pointed out the kitchen—which had been recently renovated. They walked through the downstairs gallery of portraits. Nick stopped before the portrait of her great-grandfather, Walter Ambrose, for several moments.

"This is the man who started it all," Lauren said. "When my great-grandfather found oil on the estate, everything changed."

Then they headed out the back doors and into the gardens. The warm afternoon sun had cast a lazy spell across the flowering trees and bushes. The humming of bees only added to the effect.

"It's beautiful out here," Nick said, his low voice rippling through Lauren.

She already missed him, and he hadn't even left yet.

He released her hand and stopped in front of the gazebo. She watched him examine the arching wooden beams, noticing the small things about him. The olive coloring of his skin. The set of his sturdy shoulders. The bits of whiskers that had appeared with the advancing afternoon. The quirk of his lips—those lips that she'd kissed plenty. The way he smiled at her.

She turned away, her stomach tumbling with butterflies. What if she asked him to stay? Told him how she really felt?

Walking in the direction of the family cemetery, she didn't wait for him to catch up. She was sure he would soon enough, but she needed a few moments to herself.

Lauren had been alone for thirty years, and she could conceivably continue on for decades more, living her life as it was now. Focusing on her art. Avoiding the wealthy. Enjoying peace.

Yet . . . she reached the outer wrought-iron gate that led into the graveyard. The shade here was deep, providing much-needed relief from the Texan sunshine. She heard, rather than saw, Nick approaching. His footsteps scattered a few small pebbles.

She stopped in front of the headstone that read *Richard Jacob Millet*. Lauren's grandfather and Lillian's husband. Lauren had never met him, of course, and when Nick stopped next to her, she said, "My grandfather died when he was forty. He was fishing during the spring, when the water levels were higher than normal. My grandmother said that he fell into the creek, and he became trapped under the rocks."

He listened, then said, "Does your grandmother know about the journal?"

"Yes," Lauren said. "Sofia showed it to her as well, but of course it's too late for her to do anything about it."

Nick nodded and slipped his hands into his pockets.

Lauren wished he had taken her hand, but she couldn't expect that of him now. He moved to another gravestone several paces away. The name on it read *George Frederick Ambrose II*. "This is the one whose wife wrote the journal, huh?"

"Yeah," Lauren said in a faint voice.

The wind stirred the tree branches above, and it gave a nice reprieve of cooler air. She watched Nick as he walked among the other headstones, scattered throughout the designated burial site. He didn't seem upset or annoyed, just . . . resigned. Which almost made her feel worse.

Lauren walked to a metal bench that had been painted a dark red at one point but was now more of a mottled rust color. She sat on one end and closed her eyes, letting the breeze stir her hair and cool off her neck.

She thought of all that had led her to this point. Nick's business-partner offer to her grandmother, him seeking her out in San Diego, and then . . . coming to Ambrose again to read her great-grandmother's words.

When she opened her eyes, Nick walked over to her great-grandmother's headstone and stood gazing down at it, looking deep in thought.

She knew she'd never forget that image of him—his hands in his pockets, his handsome profile somber, his hair stirring with the wind.

Suddenly, he lifted his gaze as if he'd just realized she was still there with him. His hazel eyes scanned her face, then moved lower. When his gaze returned to her face, he said, "I should go." The gentleness in his tone was mixed with a finality that made Lauren feel hollow.

She rose to her feet, her entire body trembling. Yet she took a steadying breath and moved toward Nick.

He met her halfway, and then he leaned down and kissed her cheek without touching any other part of her body. The kiss was brief, barely there, and Nick had straightened and moved away before Lauren could react. He was leaving. And she wasn't doing anything to stop him.

Her heart raced as she watched him walk away. *Do something,* she told herself. But her arms remained by her side, her feet immovable, her voice silent.

Nick continued through the cemetery until he reached the gate that had automatically swung shut on its own. He opened the gate and stepped through. He closed the gate gently, then he cast a final glance at her.

Lauren's heart nearly leapt out of her chest, and she felt like calling after him. But she didn't.

Nick gave the smallest of nods, then walked away.

Away from Ambrose. And out of her life.

Lauren didn't know how long she sat on the bench in the cemetery. She supposed she was in a bit of a shock. She'd only known Nick for a few weeks, yet he was the first man she'd imagined a future with. The first man who made her truly feel misery over the curse in her family.

She hadn't even heard his rental car drive away. No doubt he was long gone by now. Possibly even on a flight already. Maybe even a private chartered jet. He'd offered to fly her on one here, but she'd quickly turned him down.

Nick had been more than patient with her. He'd been a gentleman from the moment they stood on the airport curb together. He'd praised and respected her art. He'd even spent thousands on her paintings, for heaven's sake.

And still, Lauren sat on the metal bench. Doing nothing. It was like her soul had fled to be replaced with mechanical parts. She felt nothing. Thought nothing.

"There you are," Sofia said, her voice seeming far away.

But when Lauren looked up, her sister was standing right in front of her. Soon Sofia was settled onto the bench.

Lauren waited for her sister to speak her mind, to offer a reprimand, but Sofia simply gazed over the cemetery, and a quietness settled between the two sisters.

"Is he gone?" Lauren said at last.

"Yes." Sofia smoothed back some hair from her face.

The wind hadn't let up, but Lauren didn't mind. "Do you think I did the right thing?"

Sofia cast her a side glance. "For now. You need to be sure. And when you're sure, you'll do the *next* right thing."

24

Three Weeks Later

"MOTHER," NICK SAID, answering the phone. "Can I call you back in a few minutes? I'm in the middle of—"

"They can wait," his mother snapped. "This *can't*. Reisa Benson told me you haven't RSVP'd for her daughter's beach wedding. I told her she must be kidding, because last week you said you had."

Nick exhaled. "I said that I would as soon as I . . ." He shook his head. "I forgot, plain and simple. But I'm sure they're mostly looking forward to seeing you and not me."

"Nicholas Matthews, that's not true," his mother said. "The Bensons are your father's oldest friends, and it's imperative that we support their family on this important date."

Nick rubbed his forehead, trying to stave off the instant headache that had formed. He was drowning in work right now, since the tech company he'd hired to implement the contract for the Ambrose project had lost a key engineer, and now everyone was scrambling to make the deadlines.

"When is it?" he asked, hoping that his frustration wouldn't be detected by his mother. That would only make her more upset.

His mother hissed through her teeth. "Tonight at seven. It's a sunset wedding."

Nick closed his eyes. The timing was terrible. Yes, the Bensons went back with his family a long way, but he wasn't interested in socializing. It had been three weeks since he walked out of the

Ambrose family cemetery. Three weeks since he'd seen or heard from Lauren.

Nick hated to admit it, but he'd allowed himself to build up hope, to fall in love with a woman who he thought might love him in return, and now . . . he realized he'd been too idealistic. Lauren Ambrose had never given her heart to anyone. Her world, her simple unfettered life, centered around her art. Nick had known it from the beginning.

Nick had no reason to feel blindsided. Yet he felt exactly that. He'd allowed himself to be swept away by Lauren Ambrose. And the fall back to earth had hurt more than he could imagine.

But he couldn't hide out forever; his mother had made that more than clear.

He was still a Matthews, and he still needed to honor his father's memory. Tonight Nick would be focused on that. It was time to stop wallowing in his own misguided decisions.

Nick spent the next hour replying to emails, then sending a list of to-dos to his executive assistant. Everything else would have to wait until after the beach wedding. He'd stick to a single glass of champagne so that he could be clear-minded enough to continue working when he returned.

Finally, Nick did a search on his email to pull up the original invitation and was happy to see that the event was casual. He wouldn't have to worry about wearing a stuffy tux. He opted for khakis and a pale-green, button-down shirt that he could roll up the sleeves on. As he slipped on an older pair of Italian-leather loafers that could withstand a little sand and salt, he thought of what Lauren might say about him dressing down.

He found himself whistling as he left his house and entered the garage. He truly hoped that things with her would be well. She deserved happiness as much as the next person, and he wished her the best of whatever form that took.

The drive to the designated beach took less than ten minutes, and from the moment Nick arrived, he was glad he'd come. Several of his father's acquaintances were there, and it was like a healing balm for Nick to talk about his dad with people who knew him well.

A huge canopy had been set up. Trellis stands decorated with ivy and flowers created the sides, with the back of the tent opened to the setting sun on the Pacific. Nick had to admit, it was a very nice view. A dozen rows of chairs were arranged for the guests, and small tables were scattered about, with glowing candles surrounded by protective glass.

His mother sailed over in a sheath dress and glittery makeup. After kissing him, she said, "Barb's here, and she's dying to see you."

Nick wanted to melt into the crowd and avoid Barb at all costs. As a fifty-something woman, Barb had no qualms about showing her interest in Nick. And . . . there she was.

"Nick, honey," she crooned.

He wondered how many times she'd had plastic surgery. Maybe even she'd lost count. Not a wrinkle in sight.

"Hello, Barbara," Nick said. "Sorry I can't chat. I've got to speak with someone before they leave."

Her tweezed brows pulled together. "Who would want to leave before the ceremony?"

Nick smiled, shrugged, and moved past her. He meandered through the crowd, finding other people to chat with, and by the time it was almost time for the ceremony, he sat on the back row.

Alcohol was already being consumed, and the laughter and joviality grew with the passing moments. Nick was more than content to be sitting out of the way of the crowd, and when the pastor stood at the front of the gathering to announce the imminent ceremony, everyone took their seats.

Most of the rows in front of him were filled, but there were still a few open seats on the back row by him. And when a woman slipped into a seat two away from him, Nick didn't look over at first.

But when she crossed her legs, his peripheral vision caught a glimpse of her sandals. Ones that Nick remembered Lauren wearing. He subtly glanced over at the woman two seats down, and sure enough, Lauren Ambrose had come late to the wedding.

His first question was, what was she doing here? His second, how did she know the Bensons? She didn't appear to be with a date, and Nick didn't want to analyze the relief he felt about that. Although if Lauren was back to her serial dating, it was no business of his anyway.

He tried to focus on the ceremony, but his attention kept straying to Lauren. She wore a light-yellow dress with thin straps and a low-cut back. With her leaning forward, he could see her without her noticing him. But he really shouldn't be staring at the elegant line of her neck, the blush pink of her lips, or the way her hair was pulled into a loose chignon.

She was beautiful. As always.

Nick gave up on listening to the wedding ceremony, and as soon as it concluded and the applause began, he rose and slipped away. He didn't return to his car but took off his shoes and headed along the beach toward an outcrop of rocks. The setting sun shimmered orange against the golden horizon, and he tried to focus on the beauty of the evening and not the tumult of feelings that had risen upon seeing Lauren.

From afar, he watched the celebration of dancing and food as twilight descended. The music drifted in his direction, accompanied by laughter.

He should head back home and return to work, but he continued sitting on a wide rock and gazing out to the sea, watching the sun slip completely below the horizon and darkness replace it. The moon hung heavy in the sky, and the stars created a brilliant patchwork. Laughter and music floated from the wedding party, but Nick ignored it all.

So when someone tapped him on his shoulder, he started.

"Sorry," Lauren said. "I didn't mean to startle you."

Nick turned to look at her, unsure if he was imagining her presence. Although there was plenty of light from the moon and the wedding party, Lauren was silhouetted against the light and he couldn't see her expression.

"Do you know the Bensons?" he asked.

"Yeah, Mrs. Benson goes way back with my grandmother," Lauren said in a breathless tone. "She's originally from Texas."

"I didn't know that." Nick scooted over on the rock. He figured he'd give her room to sit, and it would be up to her to do so. "Tired of the party?"

She didn't answer for a moment as she gazed out over the dark waves undulating a few yards away. The yellow of her dress was a pale gold beneath the moonlight, and even from his place on the rock and despite the ocean breeze, her wildflower scent reached him. Taunting his senses with memories.

He hadn't realized he was holding his breath until she sat on the other edge of the rock, about two feet from him. Exhaling slowly, he tried to talk himself into remaining nonchalant. Maybe she wanted to talk about his partnership with Ambrose Oil.

"I saw your mother," she said.

So, not about the oil business. "Yeah?"

"I don't think she remembered who I was," Lauren said. "I said hello, and she smiled at me like I was a friend."

Nick shook his head at the irony. "She very well knows who you are, but my mother can be two-faced. In a crowd of people, she tends to be very pleasant."

"Hmm," Lauren said. "That was my second conclusion."

Nick hated how his mother acted sometimes and even more how she'd treated Lauren at the gala. "I'm sorry about my mother." He felt the old anger returning, but what was he supposed to do at this point? He hadn't even expected to see Lauren again.

"Your mother's not *you*, Nick," Lauren said. "You don't have to apologize for her. Besides, I can stand up for myself—believe me, women who flaunt their wealth don't bother me. Next time I see her, I'll just remind her who I am again, and we'll go from there."

Nick stared at her, although her gaze was still on the ocean. "*Next time?*"

She lifted one of her elegant shoulders in a small shrug. Then she turned her head to look at him. A soft smile played on her face, but her gaze was vulnerable. "That would depend on you."

The words were quiet, and Nick wasn't even sure he'd heard her right. "What depends on me?"

"Everything depends on you."

Her gaze held his, and a flicker of hope began in his belly, but he didn't want to trust in that hope and let it spread. "I didn't know I had so much power, because the last time I saw you, it was clear that nothing depended on me."

Her lips parted, and she slowly exhaled. "Well, you were wrong, Nicholas Matthews."

Nick wanted to kiss her, as foolish as it sounded. But they were broken up. He wasn't even sure where she was going with this. Why she'd come to talk to him. Why she was looking at him like she wanted him to say something or do something. But what?

"I don't normally like to be wrong," he finally said, "but maybe I'll make an exception if you tell me what you are talking about, Lauren Ambrose."

The edge of her mouth lifted, and her gaze warmed. Nick pressed his hands on the rock on either side of him, keeping himself grounded.

"The way I see it, when I tell you something, the ball will be in your field."

And now she was speaking in riddles. "Lauren, you're killing me. Can you cut to the chase?"

Her soft laugh escaped, and despite Nick's resolve, the hope spread to his heart.

"Ever the businessman." She rose to her feet and moved toward him.

Nick could only stare as she approached. When she stood in front of him, she wasn't touching him, but his body was already reacting to her nearness, and he was pretty sure the temperature of the ocean breeze had gone up by fifteen degrees.

When she rested her hands on his shoulders, everything inside of him burst into flame.

"What if I told you that I gave away the Renoir?" she whispered.

He blinked. And his mind tried to connect her words and what they meant, truly meant. "Why would you do that?" he said in a rasp.

"To break the Ambrose curse," she said, inching closer until her legs pressed against his.

She was too near not to touch. He moved his hands to her hips and pulled her even closer. "Why do you want to break the curse?" he whispered.

He loved her smile.

And he loved her next words even more.

"So I can be with a man who needs to learn that life is not always about business deals."

Nick chuckled, then he was on his feet, pulling her against him. She came easily into his arms, and he didn't wait another second before he claimed her mouth. Her lips were cool with the breeze, but her mouth was warm and welcoming. He moved his hands behind her back as he kissed her thoroughly, tightening his hold because he didn't plan to let her go anytime soon.

Lauren kissed him back, wrapping her arms about his neck and pushing her fingers into his hair. She tasted better than he remembered, and he decided it was time to make new memories. He trailed kisses along her jaw, then down her neck, reveling in the warmth and smoothness of her skin. When he kissed her throbbing pulse at the base of her neck, he lingered, inhaling her wildflower scent.

She skimmed her fingers across the back of his neck. "So are we back together, Nicholas Matthews?"

Nick smiled against her skin. "Absolutely, sweetheart."

Her laugh was soft. "I thought you'd put up a little more resistance than this."

"Nope."

She nestled against him, and for a moment they remained in that embrace.

"What changed your mind?" Nick asked, needing to know, deserving to know.

Her answer was one simple word. "Love."

25

It was strange walking into the gallery, knowing her Renoir was forever gone from Freddie's safe. Lauren had donated the piece to the Art Institute of Chicago, and she hoped that it might bring others happiness. She'd painted night and day when Nick had left her in Ambrose, so she had another dozen paintings finished and ready for display.

And until the moment she'd seen Nick at the Bensons' wedding, she'd wondered if she'd be alone the rest of her life. Yes, she'd decided to do the one thing to break the curse, which would allow her to not fear a premature death of her husband should she ever marry, but she couldn't imagine herself with anyone other than Nick. And if he wouldn't take her back, then she might as well become a hermit. A prolific artist hermit.

But from the instant she saw a man walking away from the wedding party, she knew it was Nick, and she knew she had to let him know what she'd done. How much she needed him. How much she loved him. How he'd become her everything.

And now she had another evening ahead of her of shaking hands, accepting congratulations and compliments, and hopefully selling a few pieces. Knowing that others loved and appreciated her art fulfilled her in ways that nothing else could. Yet her life was much fuller with Nick, in ways that she could have never predicted. The weight of the curse was gone, and until it was gone, she hadn't realized how crippling it had been, both emotionally and physically.

Lauren was the only other person in the gallery, and she could hear Freddie talking on the phone from his office, since the door was ajar. She wandered around the main room and gazed at the displays Freddie had carefully set up. Her older work was mixed in with her new paintings, and it made a nice contrast.

She paused before a painting she'd done specifically for Nick. He'd be stopping by tonight, and she wanted to see if he'd single it out. The scene was of a seashore, lit by moonlight, with two swans riding the crest of the incoming tide. She gazed at the image for a long moment, thinking of how being with Nick had made her feel like she'd undergone the transformation from the ugly duckling into a swan. Not in a physical sense but in her soul and heart.

After several moments, she moved to another display.

Freddie came out of his office. "Sorry I kept you waiting." He pulled her into a hug, then drew away. "You look marvelous."

"So do you," Lauren said, although she was flattered by the compliment. She wore a floor-length black dress, with a slit that reached above her knee. The back dipped to her waist, and she'd had her hair done professionally in an elegant twist. Her usual pendant hung on a chain about her neck.

Freddie trilled a laugh. "Don't try to deflect my compliment." He leaned close and lowered his voice. "That dress is to die for. I can't wait to see Nick's expression when he walks in."

Lauren had filled Freddie in on her progressing relationship with Nicholas Matthews. And interestingly enough, Freddie hadn't seemed surprised in the least and had only commented that he knew something was up when Nick had bought all those paintings.

"Speaking of the devil," Freddie murmured, looking past Lauren toward the entrance of the gallery.

Lauren turned to see Nick opening the door, carrying a huge vase full of roses. He wore a black tuxedo and looked like he'd stepped out of a photo shoot for the sexiest bachelor of the decade.

"Wow," Freddie said under his breath.

Wow, indeed. Lauren stared as Nick walked toward her with a smile.

"You're early." Her face heated at her lame statement.

Nick didn't seem to mind. "I brought the decorations."

When he reached her, she leaned in to smell the roses. *Heavenly.* "Thank you, they're beautiful." She met those hazel eyes of his, so warm and so intent on her.

He was still smiling. "You're welcome." Then he leaned closer and kissed her on the mouth.

Since their reunion a couple of weeks ago at the beach, Nick hadn't held back in the PDA department. No matter where they were, he was never shy about showing his affection. And Lauren wouldn't have it any other way.

Freddie cleared his throat as the kiss grew into something more than a peck. "I'll take the flowers and find a good spot."

Nick relinquished the flowers but didn't stop kissing Lauren. In fact, once both his hands were free, he slipped them around her waist and pulled her flush against him. Lauren had little choice but to twine her arms about his neck to enjoy his deliciousness.

"There," Freddie said rather loudly from across the room. "Now everyone will see the flowers the moment they enter the gallery."

Lauren broke away from Nick, first to breathe and second to thank Freddie. "They look great there, thanks."

Freddie nodded, his face a bit flushed.

Then Nick turned his head and lifted his chin at Freddie, as if he wanted him to leave the room. "Can you give us a moment, Freddie?"

What was he doing? Freddie was the gallery owner, and patrons would start arriving in ten minutes.

"I think we need to cool things down, Romeo," Lauren said when Freddie returned to his office, because Nick had pulled her back in his arms.

"Not yet," he murmured, placing a kiss right below her earlobe.

The brush of his chin against her neck tickled, and Lauren shivered with the warmth spreading through her. If she didn't break things off, then she was sure the patrons would notice her flushed cheeks and swollen lips. "Nick, I'm serious."

He lifted his head and gazed into her eyes.

Something about the intensity of his gaze made her belly heat and butterflies tumble around like mad. "Why are you looking at me like that?"

He didn't answer, but his gaze dropped to her mouth, then moved back up to meet her eyes. "I love you," he whispered.

Lauren stared at him. She couldn't explain the buzzing sensation moving through her body, and it wasn't just what Nick had said, it was how she could see it in his eyes. Leaving no doubt. With her heart hammering like mad, she whispered back, "I love you too."

He grinned and pulled her against him in a bear hug. The air practically whooshed out of Lauren, and she couldn't help but laugh.

"Good," Nick's deep voice rumbled against her ear. "Because I need to ask you something."

The butterflies were back, but Lauren didn't have time to decipher what he was saying because he pulled away and grasped one of her hands. Then he knelt on the floor in front of her.

Her eyes burned with tears, and her throat went dry.

Nick hadn't broken his gaze, even as he reached into his pocket and pulled out something round and glittery. When he held up a diamond ring, Lauren was pretty sure her knees were about to buckle.

"Lauren . . ." he began, his smile widening. "I love you more than life itself. And if you don't say yes to marrying me, then I'm going to ask you every day until you do."

She laughed, then she blinked back her tears, but it was too late. They'd already fallen.

He was watching her. Waiting.

She was pretty sure if it was physically possible, her heart would have pounded out of her chest from so much happiness. She leaned down and pressed a kiss on Nick's beautiful mouth. Then she whispered, "Yes, I'll marry you."

Nick cradled her face and deepened the kiss while he moved to his feet.

Lauren wrapped her arms about his waist and kissed him back while her heart soared and her mind raced. This was really happening. She was an engaged woman.

Clapping interrupted their kissing, and Lauren smiled against Nick's mouth as Freddie walked into the gallery.

"I'm so happy for you two," he said, still clapping. "Congratulations."

Lauren laughed and released Nick. She turned to embrace Freddie, the dear man.

Then Nick shook his hand, but Freddie said, "Oh no, you're family now," and promptly pulled him into a back-slapping hug.

"I'm opening the champagne right now," Freddie announced and hurried away to do just that.

Lauren turned back to Nick, and he ran his thumb along her jaw. "I love you."

She felt like her heart might burst. "I love you."

He grinned. "Do you want to try on the ring?"

"Of course."

Nick grasped her hand and slipped on the most gorgeous emerald-cut diamond ring she'd ever seen.

"I don't even want to ask how much you spent," she murmured.

"You're worth every penny," Nick whispered and kissed her temple.

Lauren sighed and tilted her hand so that the diamond reflected the lights of the gallery. "What will your mother say?"

"You'll find out soon enough," he said. "She's coming tonight."

Lauren's gaze flew to Nick's. "What? Here?"

Nick only smiled. "Don't worry. I think she's had a change of heart."

"Did you threaten her or something?"

Nick's smile stayed innocent. "Nothing like that." He linked their fingers and slid his other hand up her back. "I just told her that I was in love with you and that if you agreed, we'd be getting married soon."

Laruen narrowed her eyes. "What was *her* response?"

"She's coming around," he said. "But believe me, our marriage will always be between the two of us. *You and me.* No one else. Okay?"

Lauren nodded. Was it possible to love Nicholas Matthews even more?

"Here we are," Freddie said, reappearing. "I think a toast is in order."

From then on out, the time sped forward as the first patrons arrived. It was the busiest that Lauren had ever experienced, and both she and Nick were swept into conversations. But he was always close, always within sight. More than once, she felt his hand at the small of her back.

When Penny Matthews entered the gallery, Lauren noticed immediately. Her turquoise evening gown was hard to miss, and when their gazes locked, there was both a challenge and acceptance in her eyes.

Lauren stared right back.

Then Penny smiled, and Lauren knew it was genuine.

"Let me see the ring," Penny said when she reached Lauren.

The demand probably should have bothered Lauren, but it didn't. She'd proudly show off her ring from Nick to anyone, especially his mother.

Penny turned Lauren's hand side to side, then nodded. "It's lovely. My son did well."

"I agree," Lauren said.

The two women's eyes locked again.

"Thanks for coming tonight," Lauren said.

Penny nodded.

"Hello, Mother." Nick's voice rumbled near Lauren, and his hand slid around her waist.

"Nick," his mother said with a smile. "Congratulations, you two."

At that moment, Lauren saw the wistfulness in the woman's eyes. And it struck her that after Penny's divorce from his father, Nick had been the only man in her life. And now . . . she was giving that up, in a way.

Lauren's heart softened yet again. Things might not be perfect with her mother-in-law to be, but they had the common ground of Nick, and that was all that mattered.

"I'll just look around," Penny said. "Have some champagne. You know, admire the artwork."

Lauren smiled. "Enjoy yourself."

As Penny walked away, Nick pulled Lauren closer and whispered in her ear, "Thank you, sweetheart."

"Any time," Lauren said with a smile.

Then Nick stilled. "What's that?"

She followed his gaze to where the painting with the two swans hung on the wall.

"It's us."

Nick moved his arm from her waist and linked their hands, then drew her along with him to examine the painting. For several long moments, he gazed at it. "I love it."

"Good." She squeezed his hand. "Because it's for you."

He looked down at her, his eyes twinkling. "Do I have to buy it?"

"I'll give you a discount."

He chuckled, then his gaze grew more intense. "When can we get out of here? I'm tired of sharing you with people."

She placed a hand on his chest. "Soon."

The *soon* ended up becoming another ninety minutes, and by the time Lauren walked into her condo with Nick, she felt like she'd lived two lifetimes. So much had happened, but she wasn't ready to say good night to Nick yet.

When she flipped on the living room light, she stopped so suddenly that Nick bumped into her. He immediately grasped her hips to steady her.

"What . . ." His voice died.

There, mounted on the living room wall above her couch, was the Renoir painting.

"Impossible," she breathed. She moved forward quietly, as if she was afraid it might disappear if she made too much noise.

"Where did it come from?" Nick asked.

"I have no idea." Lauren stopped in front of the painting. It occurred to her that it might be a replica, but gazing at it closely, she knew it was the same one she'd donated to Chicago.

"I wonder if there was a problem and the museum returned it?" Lauren mused aloud. "But how did it get on my wall?"

"Stay here," Nick said. "I'm going to check the back rooms for any intruders."

While Nick was gone, Lauren continued to stare at the painting, wracking her mind with possibilities, but she kept coming up empty.

Nick returned and reported that he'd checked the closets, under the bed, but found nothing and no one lurking.

"I'm calling Sofia," Lauren said. "She's the only other one who knew about me donating the painting." Thankfully Sofia answered the phone, and after Lauren explained that she had a priceless painting on her wall, Sofia simply exhaled.

"What?" Lauren asked. "What is it?"

Then Sofia laughed.

"She's laughing," Lauren said to Nick. "I think she's gone crazy—me too." Then she returned to her phone call. "Sofia, I'm putting the phone on speaker. Nick's here, and you can explain what's going on. How did you get into my apartment in the first place?"

"It wasn't me, I swear," Sofia protested, her voice coming through the speaker now. "It's the curse, Lauren. It's been fulfilled. The return of the painting is a confirmation of it." She lowered her voice. "I just didn't want to share that part in case for you it was different."

"In case the painting wasn't returned?" Lauren clarified.

"Right."

Lauren went quiet, thinking. She still couldn't wrap her mind around it. "So you didn't bring it over to my place?"

"I'm in Ambrose," Sofia deadpanned.

"But . . . why would the museum suddenly send it back? Without my request?"

"I don't exactly understand either," Sofia said. "But it happened, and now you know."

Lauren asked Sofia a few more questions, but everything was coming up a dead end. According to Sofia, Lauren should just be grateful the curse had ended once and for all.

"Oh, and by the way, I heard the good news," Sofia said. "Congratulations to the both of you."

Lauren's mind did a one-eighty. "How did you know?"

"I follow Freddie on Instagram," Sofia said. "It's the only way a big sister can track her younger sister sometimes."

"Smart woman," Nick teased. "And thank you, Sofia. I hope you approve."

"Oh, I do," Sofia said with a laugh. "It's about time, in my opinion."

"I agree," a crackly voice said into the phone, surprising Lauren.

"Granny?" Lauren and her sister said at the same time.

"Don't tell me you're surprised," Lillian Ambrose said. "How do you think I became such a good businesswoman in the first place? I spent years eavesdropping on men's conversations."

Nick wrapped an arm about Lauren's shoulders and kissed her cheek. She leaned against him. "So you don't mind your future grandson-in-law being Nicholas Matthews?" Lauren asked.

"I'm delighted," her grandmother said. "Truly."

"Thank you, Mrs. Ambrose," Nick said, emotion in his voice.

Lauren felt like crying too.

"That's *Lillian* to you, Nicholas," her grandmother commanded in an amused tone. "Give me a great-grandchild, and you can call me Grandmother."

Nick chuckled and pulled Lauren closer. "I don't have a problem with that."

But Lauren was blushing. "Grandma. You can't say that."

"I already did, dear," her grandmother said. "Now these old bones are worn out from all this eavesdropping. Good night, everyone."

After hanging up with Sofia and their grandmother, Lauren wrapped both arms about Nick's waist. "I still don't get it. How did the painting get here?"

He kissed the top of her head. "I don't know, but I'm not worried about it."

"I need to check something," she said and drew away from Nick to look at her phone again. She tried to pull up the emails exchanged between herself and the Chicago museum, but nothing came up in a search.

"Hang on," she said, and she opened the laptop on her kitchen table. She did the same searches, but still nothing. She browsed her sent file, then her deleted file. There was no record of any correspondence between her and the museum. It was like it had never happened.

Lauren sat back in her chair. "Huh. It seems the painting has a mind of its own."

Nick placed his hands atop her shoulders and squeezed. "Maybe we can call the museum tomorrow?"

"No." Lauren rose to her feet and turned to face her new fiancé.

"I want to forget about the curse once and for all. From this moment on, I think I need to focus more on the amazing man in my life."

Nick's brows rose, and his lips curved into a smile. "Oh? Really? And how are you planning on doing that?"

"I think kissing you is a good start."

Nick chuckled, and as his laughter faded, his gaze grew serious again. "Did I tell you I love you?"

"A few times." She moved her hands up his chest and looped her arms about his neck. "But you can tell me again."

His hands slid around her waist, then he anchored her against him, and before kissing her again, he whispered, "I love you, Lauren Ambrose."

MORE BOOKS IN THE WOMEN OF AMBROSE ESTATE SERIES:

Heather B. Moore is a four-time *USA Today* bestselling author. She writes historical thrillers under the pen name H.B. Moore; her latest thrillers include *The Killing Curse* and *Breaking Jess*. Under the name Heather B. Moore, she writes romance and women's fiction. Her newest releases include the contemporary sports romances, Belltown Six Pack series, and the small town romance series Pine Valley. She's also one of the coauthors of the *USA Today* bestselling series: Timeless Romance Anthologies. Heather writes speculative fiction under the pen name Jane Redd; releases include the Solstice series, *Mistress Grim,* and *Midsummer Night.* Heather is represented by Dystel, Goderich & Bourret.

For book updates, sign up for Heather's email list:
hbmoore.com/contact
Amazon Author Page: Heather B. Moore
Website: HBMoore.com
Facebook: Fans of H. B. Moore
Blog: MyWritersLair.blogspot.com
Instagram: @authorhbmoore
Twitter: @HeatherBMoore

www.ingramcontent.com/pod-product-compliance
Lightning Source LLC
LaVergne TN
LVHW021821060526
838201LV00058B/3471